BT

Count the Dead

Dawson is thrown off a freight train, half-dead. Then, when he finally finds himself riding into a nearby town, he is on a stranger's horse with a dead man roped behind the cantle.

Against all odds he finds himself a riding job with decent sidekicks. It looked good but trouble awaited him. Instead of tallying round-up steers he was forced to fight for his very life.

Count the Dead

Rick Dalmas

A Black Horse Western

ROBERT HALE · LONDON

ISBN 978-0-7090-9191-2

Robert Hale Limited
Clerkenwell House
Clerkenwell Green
London EC1R 0HT

www.halebooks.com

Typeset by
Derek Doyle & Associates, Shaw Heath
Printed and bound in Great Britain by
CPI Antony Rowe, Chippenham and Eastbourne

CHAPTER 1

NO FREE RIDE

The bullet wound in his side was bleeding again.

Damn nuisance! It was a shallow groove across a couple of ribs, dipped a little in one place; oughtn't to be bleeding so much . . . might've nicked a vein. . . .

That was a remnant of the teaching of long-ago times, but true nonetheless. He rolled heavily against the slatted wall of the cattle car as the train rounded a bend – too damn fast! whistle screeching, waking up the countryside for a mile around. Whistle-crazy engineer! They were still many miles from Durham Bend, nothing out here but wild, empty land, horizon to horizon, big cats, mustangs, wildlife.

He wadded the already bloody neckerchief and held it firmly on the wound, straining to see, intending to lay the cloth over the gouge, then push his shirt tail in tightly enough to hold it in place – if it would stay put.

He didn't get the chance to find out.

A shadow flickered down the dung-caked slats, on the outside, as someone climbed down from the roof of the swaying car. So that was what had thudded above just before the bend! A damn railroad patrol! Watching no saddlebums got a free ride.

Whoever it was knew what he was doing and had the lock released in seconds. The big slatted door rolled back like distant thunder, crashed against the stops, and a big dark shape, silhouetted against the lightening sky, swung in and landed with legs spread, growing out of big boots like young trees.

The guard hulked huge as he straightened, wearing an unbuttoned jacket, and a dusty derby hat that had seen lots of wear. He hefted a sawn-off axe-handle, slapping it into the palm of a hand that Matt Dawson reckoned he could have sat in.

Judas! Just his luck to run up against a walking mountain!

'Thought I seen a light flash earlier.' The voice was raspy, no sign of shortness of breath: this one was fit – and eager. 'Just couldn't wait for that cigarette, eh? Took the chance the match flare wouldn't be seen through the slats. Well, it was, 'cause I'm always on the lookout. Now guess what happens.'

Dawson looked up, his lean, stubbled face mostly in the shadow of the battered curlbrim hat. 'You're gonna take pity on a cowpuncher down on his luck and who's toting a wound from the derringer of a tinhorn gambler who stole my last three bucks.'

There was a wheezy sounding laugh, very short.

6

'Noticed the soggy shirt tail.' There was even a little interest in the railroad man's voice. 'Who done it?'

'The son of a bitch runs the poker concession in the saloon at Drinkwater.'

The guard grinned, not with any warmth. 'Ah, good of Cold-deck Sampson – he sure do like the bottom of them card decks, don't he?'

'Yeah. My mistake was telling him that.'

'Lucky to be alive – or are you?'

Dawson was watching that axe handle when he should have been watching the man's size fourteen boots.

One of them took him in the side, a few inches above the bullet gouge, and he felt his ribs creak as he was slammed back hard against the swaying wall. The boot swung in against his shoulders which were now towards the guard, who pinned him there with a grinding knee.

'Not your lucky day, feller. This is to tell you there ain't no free rides on this railroad!'

The club slammed across Dawson's shoulders and he grunted. Then it struck again and this time he yelled. A knee of one of those thick legs drove into the back of his head, ramming his face into the slats. Splinters ripped his skin, bent his nose, and warm blood gushed into his mouth and over his chin.

He knew damn well the season was fall, so why was someone celebrating Fourth of July with all those fireworks bursting in flares of shattering light behind his eyes?

He was still wondering when he felt several more

thumps, and bone-creaking agony writhed through him like fire. That damn boot kept drumming into his back, working up and down his spine. He was half-paralysed, pinned and confined.

Just as if he was at the bottom of a well, he heard these words, hollow-sounding, yet clear enough:

'Your boots look OK, feller. You'll be able to walk for miles before the soles give out – or you do. With a little luck you might even make Durham, but I kinda doubt it. Still, you're a gamblin' man, it seems, so this is the hand you're bein' dealt. Lots of luck, saddle-bum!'

Through his half-consciousness he felt the grip on his shirt collar – it almost strangled him – then a second set of banana fingers closed around his belt. The thin leather strap felt as if it was cutting him in two as he began to swing back and forth, back and forth. Just two swings and the cold air of early morning cleared his reeling senses enough for him to know he was flying now. *Flying!*

Not far, though. Before long there was a rapid falling sensation, a glimpse of hard, gravel-studded ground rushing towards him.

Although the sun was barely peeping over the mountain in the east, it went suddenly dark, shot through with jarring, body-racking thud. Then it was night again.

Black, impenetrable night.

He sat on a rock, senses still whirling, arm pressed into his left side, trying to hold the sodden kerchief over the wound again. It wasn't bleeding quite so much, which surprised him after his rough exit from the freight train.

He ached and throbbed from scalp to toenails, had picked up a slew of scrapes and cuts and bruises.

Still, he was mostly alive and he had his sack of tobacco. But the pocket was torn and all his vestas had spilled out, so he petulantly threw away the lumpy cigarette he had just rolled, accompanying the action with a string of curses that could've only been learned by years of riding the cattle trails.

He groaned as the brief, violent action pulled at bruised muscles and over-stretched tendons, and diverted a few of those curses to the man who had beaten him up. He'd know him again. Fact, he thought he knew who he was already: a railroad buster called 'Deadwood', prowling the freight trains, looking for free-loaders and enjoying beating the hell out of them before throwing them off the moving train.

'I'd been hopin' to cross your trail for a long time, you son of a bitch,' Dawson growled into the still cool morning. 'But we'll meet again. Bet your life on it.'

There wouldn't be another train going north or south for at least three days by his calculation. In that time, he ought to be able to make the water tanks at Scourpan, if he didn't die of thirst or heatstroke meantime, or his injuries were worse than he thought.

Wouldn't matter even if a train came through now, come to think of it; wasn't likely it would stop just because some ragged-ass drifter flagged it down. . . .

9

So, as usual, it was up to himself to get out of this bind.

Start walking and quit feelin' sorry for yourself!

Just thinking of all that water at the tanks had sparked his already raging thirst. But Scourpan was a long, long way off yet.

And it wasn't even likely he could reach the tanks.

His hat sat well enough but his nose was swollen and clogged with dried blood. Breathing through his mouth dried the parched membranes even more and his cut tongue felt like it was already swelling.

'Man, you are a misery! Will you, for Chris'sakes, get moving!'

He stopped and looked at the sky, still writhing with sun-emblazoned clouds, and felt a lump of lead in his belly as big as a boot. The day was just starting! And this wasn't what you would call a good beginning; how it was going to end was probably more important.

This time he began to move, staggering steps, sliding on the gravel, arms flapping like a wounded bird in his efforts to stay balanced. He was surprised to find his six-gun was still in its scarred holster; that was what must have given him such a wallop on his right hip when he landed.

Swaying, he checked the loads and for any damage. Nothing critical; he had the notion suddenly that he could pull a bullet from a cartridge, then fire the gun into a handful of dry grass or dead-leaf tinder, and he'd have a fire. But nothing to cook, you idiot!

He sighed. 'You're a pain in your own ass! Where's the profit in this? Finding more things to worry about!

Get on with it! You do what you can. If it ain't enough, why, you just keep on doin' it; there's no other choice.'

Maybe his pep-talk to himself stirred some effort for he slid down the rest of the slope, glimpsing a thin banner of smoke way, way ahead and off to his left: the damn train! So he hadn't been out to the wide world all that long.

Come on! Move while it's still reasonably cool.

It was time to find out what he was made of.

There was at least one big mountain to cross and when he saw it looming up just after high noon, the glare rasping at his eyes, making his skin cower and shrivel, his already shaky legs trembled even more. Mother Mountain was what they called it, if he had his location fixed correctly. Highest one in this neck of the woods. Naturally!

But then he paused; the railroad had tunnelled *through* it during construction! Man, if he could make it that far, the cool, dark shelter of the tunnel would refresh him. Might even be some pools of water that hadn't evaporated since the last rain, or oozing out of the earthen walls!

The promise – no, the *possibility* – that he might find at least temporary salvation there lent him more strength that he'd believed he possessed, and he staggered on through the man-killing heat.

The rest of the day passed in a blur – a series of blurs, for he fell countless times, crawled to the meagre shade of some nearby boulder or straggly bush to rest up a spell, let his thudding heart settle; then he started over.

His tongue was filling his mouth now, or, leastways, that was how it felt. His belly was scraping his backbone; must be at least two days since he had eaten. His muscles were knotting in cramps on the slopes. He was half-blind with the glare, kept his eyes pinched down as much as possible.

Then, sometime during the afternoon, his head buzzing with strange sounds, he saw the cutting in the lower slopes of Mother Mountain – the cutting leading into the raw hillside and the gaping black maw of the tunnel. Beckoning.

Dawson didn't remember making it into the tunnel, but he sure remembered that first pool of black water just a few yards inside, glinting with reflected sunlight. He fell to aching knees, scooped up a handful, straining dead insects and floating rubbish through his fingers. His teeth filtered out other muck and the water tasted . . . like engine oil! Must be excess spewed from a locomotive. He vomited it back up with whatever little else had been, in his belly, but it didn't matter. Better out than in.

It shook him badly. Resting against the curved side of the tunnel, the letdown starting to work on him now, he sat and watched the daylight fade. The sun was setting on the far side of the mountain, so a solid, humped shadow stretched out from his side. It was going to be a long, hungry uncomfortable night, but he might stumble on fresh water trickling down from the roots of trees on the mountainside further into the tunnel. It was at least a mile long, if he recalled correctly, and it was all his. There were no trains calling at this station, *amigo*, so even sleep between the rails if you've a mind.

His senses dulled and he wandered off into a kind of sleep: deep, exhausted but not deep enough to stop the fingers of pain from his injuries making him moan or twitch.

It was pitch-dark when the mists began to swirl away and he blinked, realizing where he was almost immediately. His mouth was lined with something that tasted like dried cowdung – not that he remembered ever tasting cowdung! – and he belched and tried to spit, but there wasn't enough saliva.

Then he gasped and reached for his Colt as some beast moved in towards him, bulking large against the paler light of the arched entrance.

'What the hell!'

He palmed up the gun awkwardly, cocked the hammer, the spur of which had been bent a little during his fall from the train. Then he heard the whinny, the chink of harness, and he smelled horse.

Dawson froze, his reeling senses unable to grasp or believe what he was seeing. Half-seeing, in this light.

There was a saddled mount clopping towards him and enough light for him to read the brand on one hip: Lazy J.

No rider. But a water canteen was slung from the saddle horn!

He grabbed it with shaking hands, murmuring some foolishness to the horse, just to put it at ease.

Water sloshed in the metal bottle, and sloshed down his throat seconds later until he had to gasp for breath. *Easy!* Not so much at once, you damned fool! The horse nudged him twice, almost knocking him down, before he realized that it, too, needed water.

He poured a cupful into his hat, pinching the hole worn in the peak of the crown tightly to save leakage. The horse slurped it up. It was a dun gelding, a typical cow pony, with lots of dust and dirt clinging to its hide. As he reached for the saddle-bags to check for any grub, he noticed a scar on the cantle that he knew damn well, even in this dimness, had to have been made by a bullet – and not all that long ago, either.

Then, as he unbuckled the flap he saw the stirrup. There was something jammed in the arch of the iron.

A man's riding-boot was caught in there, worn, dusty – and stained with dark blood.

CHAPTER 2

WELCOME STRANGER

Durham Bend was larger than he expected, but still wasn't much.

A grey, weathered cow town used by trail herds travelling to the meathouse railhead at Sabinas. The railroad Dawson had travelled on – partly! – ended here, and a spur track ran to the copper mines at Telegraph Creek, though there was not yet a telegraph line at The Creek, as it was known. Cattle were driven in from the surrounding ranch land and railed back to the main line at Hornet Junction for shipping on to Sabinas.

So the town ought to look a mite more prosperous, Matt Dawson figured. But, as he rode the dun with its blanket-draped draped burden behind the cantle, he saw there were at least two saloons to cater for the

15

cowhands and sometimes workers at the poorly paying copper-mines. Just in case that wasn't enough to keep them happy, there was a place right on Main, with a faded sign above the awning. There was enough paint on it to show a leggy gal, holding her skirts high, about one inch short of being indecent, pursued by a wild-eyed cowboy holding his falling trousers, tongue hanging out lasciviously.

It was called Cowboy Heaven and he wondered about the law hereabouts, to allow this kind of thing on the main drag; backstreets were OK, but *Main*. . . ? Maybe it was a liberal-minded town.

Or maybe the paint was really too faded to offend, and he was just using his imagination.

Anyway, he had more to think about than the buxom wench or even raw liquor. He had a dead man roped over the weary dun's rump and folk on the boardwalks stopped to stare, a couple propping even in the middle of the street, causing the wagons and flatbeds to go around them, the drivers' curses trailing.

He called to an obvious cowpuncher seated on a set of short steps leading up to a saloon's batwings: 'Where'll I find the law?' His voice was still raspy from not enough water but his thirst would be taken care of pretty soon, he hoped.

The cowboy seemed surprised at the question, gestured with a thumb to a narrow door half a block to his right. A narrow plank above it, paint faded like the Cowboy Heaven sign, said, simply, Marshal – without any kind of illustration.

By now a small crowd was gathering. As Dawson turned the dun towards the hitchrail the law office door opened and a man came out on to the small porch. He was of average height, lean, though starting to thicken a little around the waist, and the thinning steel-grey hair probably put him in his fifties, Dawson reckoned.

'Who are you? And what've you got there?'

The marshal had a round face that looked like he could have a touch of Indian blood: flattish features, high cheekbones, hooked nose, but smaller than the normal Indian's. He had a grey moustache above a thin-lipped mouth and bushy, pepper-and-salt brows, shaded deepset dark eyes with puckered crows' feet at the corners.

It was a face that could be friendly or deadly – or somewhere in between. Like now.

'Name's Matt Dawson. Found this feller out near Mother Mountain.'

He noticed, as the lawman stepped closer, that there was a milky-blue blur of encroaching age on the whites of those penetrating eyes now fixed on Dawson's face.

'I know who your passenger is, if he belonged to that horse, but you'd better tell me how you come by it – and something about yourself, apart from your name.'

'Here?' Dawson looked around him at the gawking crowd and the bustle on the street behind him. 'I'm plumb tuckered, Marshal. I'd like to put up my horse and have a bath and a square meal. Be glad to answer

17

any question after that.'

'I already asked the question. You answer. Now.'

Dawson felt his jaw harden and figured it would likely show through the dirt and stubble, but to hell with it. If this inconsiderate damn lawman didn't like it, too bad.

He folded his hands on the saddle horn; the dun's head was drooping, rolling one eye towards a wooden trough across the street. The crowd moved closer.

'Matt Dawson, trailhand, cowpuncher, Jack of all trades on this or any other frontier. Last place I been was Drinkwater. Lost all my *dinero* to a tinhorn, jumped an empty car on a nine-car freight, but some damn railroad bully-boy figured the train was over-crowded and threw me off, with the help of a big axe-handle club. Managed to walk as far as Mother Mountain tunnel and the dun wandered in. There was a bloody boot jammed in the stirrup and enough water in the canteen to get us both this far. *Now*, can I stall the dun and. . . .'

He paused as he realized the crowd was murmuring. The marshal, staring at him bleakly, stepped down and flipped back the old blanket covering the dead man. The crowd edged closer and there was a mixture of curses and gasps.

'Yeah, he don't look too pretty,' Dawson said as the lawman lifted the head by the blood-stiff hair. 'He's been dragged a ways when his foot caught in the stirrup, but someone shot him first. If you look a mite closer, Marshal, amongst all that raw meat. . . .'

The marshal glanced up from examining the

corpse. 'I see the bullet wound – in his back,' he snapped. 'You claim you found him in this shape?'

'Not only claim it, I damn well did! Just like I already told you.'

'Get down.' The lawman wasn't armed as far as Dawson could see but he spoke as if he had a cocked shotgun backing his words. *Used to being obeyed.*

'Well, you show me where the livery is and—'

'I said "get down".' The voice wasn't raised, but there was a heap of confidence in the way the marshal spoke.

Then Dawson was mighty surprised when he felt fingers grip his lower left leg and heave.

There was enough strength in that movement – for a man past his mid-fifties – to send Dawson floundering. He clawed at the saddle horn as the dun snorted and stomped and that was it: he spilled sideways, struggling to get his feet under him, and next he knew he was standing beside the dun, groping at the saddle to help him stay upright. The marshal seemed pale and tight-lipped, idly rubbing his upper left arm.

The jostling and squirming had loosened Dawson's bloody shirt tail and it slid back to reveal the stained neckerchief hanging from the derringer wound.

'Hey!' someone close enough to make it out yelled. 'This one's got a bullet wound, too, Marshal!'

The lawman stepped around the spooked dun. Dawson was still getting his balance when a hand roughly thrust him hard enough for his boot heel to catch on the edge of the boardwalk and he sat down with a thump that dragged a moan from him.

19

The lawman leaned down swiftly and straightened just as fast, holding Dawson's six-gun, the hammer cocked.

'Judas priest! What the hell're you doin'. . . ?'

'On your feet!'

Dawson climbed up slowly, seeing a lot of hostile faces confronting him. 'Listen, *I* didn't kill that feller, whoever he is! I found him just like I said. Backtracked the dun about a mile past the tunnel – and before you ask, his pockets were already turned inside out. He'd been searched.'

'Very likely!' the lawman said sardonically. His face was hard-lined, the gun unwavering. 'Guess it'd be natural to search him, anyway. But he wouldn't've travelled far with that bullet in his back. His name's Luke Rafter and he's been missing for a couple of days.'

'Yeah, well, I'd say it could be that long since he was shot . . . and I still didn't kill him.'

The marshal said, sarcastically, 'Know about such things, do you? Can tell how long a man's been dead?'

'Sometimes. I was a field medic during the War.'

'You'd've been just a kid!'

'Fifteen when I started out. Six years later, when it ended, I was a hundred years old.'

The crowd murmured but there was just a touch more respect showing now: battlefield medics were regarded right up there with the saints and angels, nationwide, even all these years after Appomattox.

But the gun held steady on him. 'Reckon we'll let our local sawbones take a look at Luke.'

'His left forearm's missing,' Dawson pointed out,

20

getting everyone's attention in an instant. 'He was lying right alongside the railroad tracks, must've died there, one arm flung across the rails. You can see it if you flip back the blanket a little more—'

'Hell, the driver would've spotted him!' someone said curtly.

'Not if it happened at night. And, judging by the look of the splintered bone and the way the flesh is mangled, I reckon it was likely the same train as that son of a bitch threw me off that done it.'

The lawman regarded him closely. 'Giving yourself an alibi, huh?'

'I seen enough dead men during the War, Marshal, to know this feller Luke wasn't alive when the train took his arm off. Which means I was miles back down the track, nursing my own hurts, and—'

'If he was already dead, you couldn't've been the one to shoot him,' the marshal finished for him. He scowled as Dawson nodded. 'Fits a mite too neatly for my liking. Dawson, I'm gonna offer you the hospitality of my jail while I look into this some more.'

'For Chris'sake! I didn't have to bring him in here! I could've just rode away and left him – which I would've done if I'd killed him.'

'Forking Luke's horse? Sure. But you didn't do that, and now you're here and you've got to prove your story.'

'Hell, you find me that bastard Deadwood and after I'm through with him, he'll prove it by telling you just when he threw me off the train! I'll damn well guarantee that!'

'Oughtn't be too hard to find him,' spoke up a man in the front row. 'I seen the son of a bitch in Cowboy Heaven only last night, an'—'

There was a dull crack and the man's hat was knocked off. He yelped, clapping a hand over one ear, under the icy gaze of an irate, grey-haired woman standing behind him, glaring from under a faded yellow sunbonnet.

'And just what were you doing in that den of sin and degradation, Gabby Marx? Tell me that if you will!'

The crowd was chuckling and cat-calling now at the crestfallen Gabby, who was cursing his slip of the lip.

'Yeah, Gabby, how come you can afford Madam Molly's prices?'

'Where you see him? In the bar? Or up in one of them fancy lovin'-rooms I hear they got?'

'Well, you'd know Deadwood, whichever end you was lookin' at!'

'Yeah. Big 'n' ugly—'

'All right, all right, that's enough!' roared the marshal. He gestured to Dawson. 'Inside.'

'You're not going to lock me up, for God's sake!'

'I am – and I'll gunwhip you first if you don't move.' He said it hard, but Dawson thought he detected a shade of uncertainty too, which didn't seem to make sense.

Dawson clambered slowly to his feet and was prodded roughly towards the office door. The lawman was speaking as they went:

'Gabby, you take Luke down to Doc Fallon's and get that horse stalled and looked after. Rest of you go home. You'll find out soon enough whether we've got Luke's killer or not.'

CHAPTER 3

SQUARING-UP

Doc Fallon came to the cell where Dawson rested on the bunk smoking a cigarette, courtesy of the marshal, Lyndon Britt. It was a name Dawson had heard most places he had travelled, and that meant most of the country west and south of the Mississippi, as well as roundabout, across and up or down. You name it and more than likely Matt Dawson had been there.

Lyndon Britt – hell in a hand-basket twenty years ago. Town-tamer, ex-Ranger, ex-federal marshal: *hell in a hand-basket.* You bent to his law or went down to his gun or fists. Then, suddenly, you didn't hear much about him for years. These days, except maybe for some old-timer who claimed to have seen Britt in action – which, by all accounts, was something to see – his deeds were mostly legends. And, like all legends, they had stretched into the realm of fantasy. But he was older now, ailing some, judging by the sound of that cough that sawed at him now and again. But he was still a hard bastard, and wouldn't give an inch on this Luke Rafter deal.

Now he came and stood behind the stoop-shouldered medic, a man only a couple of years younger than Britt. The doctor had a lightly stained moustache and a stringy goatee. His eyes looked tired.

'They tell me you were a field medic all through the War?'

'Near enough. They put a rifle in my hands every now and then, twice stuck me behind a cannon, but mostly I was tending wounded.'

'You have any medical background?'

Dawson snorted. 'I was born on the wrong side of the blanket, Doc. Had about seven different "mothers" – or that's what the feller who claimed to be my pa called 'em. He was a trail-herder, left me with one or other of 'em most times, then started taking me along on the drives. I was roustabout, firewood gatherer, Jack-go-fetchem. Guess I had about six months' total schooling in my life before the War came along and some shavetail lieutnant passing through our town dragged me outta the crowd. Said he needed someone to run messages. Turned out he was an army surgeon and guess he liked my style 'cause he taught me about first aid and so on, gave me books with all these gory pictures of peoples' innards. Nearly threw up at first, but I got kinda interested.'

'Well, he knew what he was about, I reckon. You were right about poor Luke Rafter being dead when the train severed his forearm. Possibly dead about a day.' The doctor turned to look at the marshal. 'What's that do for him, Lyn? Get him off the hook?'

'We-ell, I guess I'd like confirmation of just when he was tossed off that train, but Deadwood's been drunk for two days straight, they tell me, and wouldn't know his own name without prompting.'

'Likely wouldn't say anything to back *me* up, anyways,' Dawson allowed.

'No,' agreed Doc Fallon. 'You know your job, Lyndon, but I'd be inclined to believe this man's story, His own bullet wound is as old as he claims, which puts it at least another day earlier than Luke's death.'

Britt frowned. 'His gun had been fired.'

'Told you!' cut in Dawson irritably. 'I used it to light a fire. No vestas, so I shot a cartridge without the bullet into dry grass. I had a lizard I tried to cook. Sizzled the blame thing and couldn't stomach it anyway.'

The medic smiled faintly. 'What d'you say, Lyndon?'

'Ah, hell. I can read a man pretty good and I had a feelin' from the start he was speakin' gospel, but . . . well, I wired the sheriff at Drinkwater and he says a gambler named Sampson was shot when a drifter accused him of four-flushing. The drifter was shot, too, name of Dalton, he thought, but mebbe he meant Dawson.'

He paused and looked quizzically at his prisoner.

'I already told you about the tinhorn. Cold-deck Sampson.'

'Did you kill him?' asked the doctor.

Britt answered. 'No, Doc. Sampson's gonna have

digestion trouble for the rest of his life, but he'll live.'

'Perhaps he'll be better for the lesson,' Fallon suggested and Britt scowled a little.

'I've still my job to do. All right, Dawson. Doc's behind you, and your story more or less checks out. I'm gonna release you, but you stick around town for a few days, just in case. I'll tell you when you can leave.'

'Can I keep that dun I brought in?'

The marshal looked at him hard. 'You sure believe in pushin' your luck, don't you?'

'I got no horse, not even my saddle. Unless Deadwood threw it off the train after me.'

'No-oo. But I heard he was forkin' a mount with a different rig from his usual one.'

Dawson, standing in the passage now, rubbing his numbed backside, looked up quickly. 'Two-tone leather? Dark seat, lighter cantle? Saddle-bags with flaps a shade lighter colour than the body. . . ?'

'Sounds about right from what I hear. I haven't seen it myself.'

'That's mine, all right! The lousy son of a bitch stole it.'

'Spoils of war, Dawson,' Britt told him coolly. 'But it does kinda back your story a little more.'

'What about the dun? I get to keep it or not?'

The medic spoke as Britt hesitated. 'Luke was a loner. I doubt there'd be anyone else to lay claim to his horse. Woman named Eadie Kern's taken over Lazy J, called Box K now.'

Britt's nod was reluctant. 'All right – but you stick

around, Dawson, like I said.'

'Er – pushing it just a mite more, Marshal, could you stake me enough for grub and a room?' As Britt drew himself up to his full height, still three inches shorter than Dawson, Matt added, quickly, 'Just till I find a job. I'll pay you back.'

Doc Fallon grinned. 'You got a petty cash allowance, Lyndon, haven't you?'

Marshal Britt sighed. 'Come on! Sooner I get you outta my jail – outta my town – the better. You already been fed one meal on the County.'

'Never touched the sides goin' down, Marshal,' Dawson told him with a half-grin. 'I'm still a growin' boy.'

'A thirty-year-old boy! Just don't keep pushin' things with me or you mightn't see thirty-one!'

Deadwood wasn't drunk, just plain mean, with one hell of a hangover, and broke into the bargain.

He asked for drinks on the house at the saloon, and amiable Tate Meehan, the owner, gave him one whiskey with a beer chaser if he wanted it.

'And that's the limit, Deadwood. You've busted up my barkeep and kicked the swamper ass-crooked. So down your drinks and move along or I'll call the marshal.'

Deadwood leaned across the bar, his ugly face uglier than ever. 'How'd you like to feel my axe-handle across your goddam head, Tate?'

Tate leaned down and brought up his sawed-off shotgun, resting the barrels on the edge of the counter. 'How'd you like my friend here to give you an argument about that?'

Deadwood eased back, mouth twisting, but the bravado didn't reach his eyes; they were mighty wary and there just might have been a faint tremor in the big hand that lifted the shotglass and tossed the raw redeye down his throat.

'There'll be a night when you're at the other end of the bar, Tate,' Deadwood growled, nodding to the shotgun.

Tate rapped the counter with the gun. 'This'n's got a few kinfolk at various places along the bar. 'Night, Deadwood. If ever you feel like comin' back – don't.'

The burly railroad guard scowled and stomped out, thrusting men aside, almost tearing one batwing off its hinges. He stepped on to the walk, feeling the night wind stirring a little dust, but it did nothing for the hangover which had not been soothed in any way by the free drink. Then he felt an urgent pressure in his bladder, stepped off the saloon veranda and lurched into the dark alley. He took maybe a dozen steps down and then tucked his pickaxe handle under one arm while he relieved himself. It was a strong pungent stream and he gave a satisfied sigh before buttoning up. He let the club drop loosely into his right hand and turned back towards Main . . . and stopped dead.

There was someone standing between him and the glow of the main street.

'Who's that?' he demanded warily, already tensing and starting to crouch. He was a man who had a lot of enemies.

'Me, you son of a bitch.'

'Who the hell's "me"?'

'You never stopped to ask my name, but it's Matt Dawson.'

'Daw—? Hell, that free-loader I tossed off the freight a few nights back?' Deadwood chuckled, grinned, teeth showing in a pale line. 'Well, smoke me for a— *Hey*! What's that you got there?'

'This?' Dawson hefted the yard-long two-by-four piece of hardwood he had picked up at a building site behind the livery after seeing to his newly acquired dun mount. 'I'm kinda poorly right now, Deadwood. Can't exert myself too much – doctor's orders. So – figured I'd even things up some.'

'You stupid saddlebum! I'll beat you to a pulp.'

The rest of the words were smashed back into his mouth as Matt Dawson swung his length of timber, right where those teeth had gleamed dully in the darkness of the alley.

Lips mashed, teeth broke, blood flowed, and Deadwood staggered back half a dozen paces, lurching off balance. Dawson stepped after him swiftly, slammed the club across the man's beefy shoulders as he bent over, spitting so he wouldn't choke on his own blood. The blow drove him to his knees and Dawson swung up the club again.

But Deadwood was a tough man, had brawled and scuffled all his life, knew every trick in the book and then some, and he was as hard as a tree-stump.

Not that he hadn't been hurt. His face felt as if it had been smashed to the back of his skull and his neck

30

tendons were on fire, his ears thundering with head noises. But he put up a big hand and grabbed Dawson's wrist just behind his grip on the club as it descended.

Matt was surprised at the way Deadwood rose to his feet, twisting his arm now. The pain was forcing his fingers to loosen their grip on the club. Deadwood spat in his face and Dawson jerked aside in revulsion. The club fell and Deadwood yanked him in close against his iron-hard body, lifted a knee. Matt twisted and took the blow on the outside of his thigh, but there was enough force in it to jerk his feet off the ground. He floundered and Deadwood threw him to the alley floor, stomped and kicked at his head with an oversize boot.

Instinct alone made Dawson wrench his head to the left. He felt the boot skid across his cheek, tear at one ear. The impact made Deadwood grunt and he lurched forward a little. Matt came up like a missile shot from a cannon and the top of his head smashed into Deadwood's already ruined face. He stumbled, spreading his boots fast in an effort to keep his balance.

That was when Dawson managed to grab his length of timber. He brought it up in an underhand blow between Deadwood's legs. The big man's scream made Dawson jump and the brutal guard collapsed, vomiting, rolling about, clasping at his crotch, making dreadful, animal-like sounds.

Matt Dawson bet there were a few dozen of Deadwood's victims who would willingly pay a hundred dollars cash just to witness this scene, right at this moment.

'Hell, Deadwood, I can't stand to see a hurt animal suffer! Better put you out of your misery.'

First, Matt swung his club into Deadwood's right collarbone. The snap was lost in his renewed screams. Then the hardwood hissed like a raging rattler on the strike and cracked Deadwood's left arm above the elbow. The last target was his bullet head and the man went limp, his big body jerking and twitching; he had a hard head, was still barely conscious.

'If you can hear me, you miserable dog's dropping, that was on behalf of a man named Mitch Curtin. But you likely wouldn't even remember. It's years since you crippled him, and it'll be almost as long before you can even roll a cigarette with those hands. You'll never ride the freights again, breaking the bones of hungry men with the backsides outta their pants. You'll be lucky if you can blow your nose.'

Men were already running into the alley, one with a lantern. As the dull orange light washed over the bloody heap on the ground, someone said,

'Anyone got a medal?'

'A medal!'

'Yeah. I'd like to pin it on the feller who done this. Fact, if he ain't too damn ugly, I might even kiss him.'

So spoke one of Deadwood's victims who happened to be living in Durham right now. He went off, limping, but whistling. Matt Dawson slipped away into the darkness, his bloody club tossed into the general trash pile in the alley.

He felt a little blood oozing from the bullet wound but it didn't bother him: he wouldn't have cared if it had burst every stitch Doc Fallon had put in.

He felt good, as he always did, after squaring up a grudge.

And this one had been binding his craw for too long a time. . . .

Which cut no ice with Marshal Lyndon Britt.

'Why come to me?' Dawson said. He was standing in his long johns beside the narrow cot in the lean-to behind the law office, where Britt had told him he could stay for a couple of nights.

'Now why wouldn't I come to you?' Britt countered. 'Hardcase with one helluva grudge agin Deadwood, who turns up in an alley with a busted face, broken collarbone, broken arm – and Doc tells me it'll be a long while before he can put his wedding tackle to the use it was designed for, if ever. Doc's gonna send him to Hornet Junction where they got a proper hospital. He'll be there a long time, Doc says.' A pause, then Britt added, with a touch of relish: 'A real long time.'

'Well, that's good news. Far as I'm concerned, I dunno who put Deadwood in that condition, but I'd sure like to shake his hand.'

Britt stepped to the end of the cot, lifted a shirt spattered with fresh blood, as too were the corduroy trousers crumpled on the floor. 'You need to do some laundry.'

'Yeah. Busted the stitches in my side, bled all over me. Doc warned me about it, but. . . .'

The marshal sighed. 'All right! I can see I won't get

far with this. But you watch yourself! I'm still not satisfied with your story about Luke Rafter. So don't try to
leave town yet.'

'Hell, no. I've got me a bed and couple bucks
thanks to your petty cash, for which I say again *muchas
gracias*. Got me a fair sort of horse and my own saddle
back. I'm happy enough way things are.'

'The way things are, you're walking a tightrope and
if it wasn't for Deadwood's reputation and the way he
beat up Tate Meehan's barkeep you'd be back behind
bars. Oh – an' did I mention we got us a chain gang,
too that could do with some more help? Meantime,
get some sleep. Then start lookin' for work, so you can
make my petty cash balance again.'

'I aim to do that, Marshal. And – thanks.'

'Nothin' to thank me for. I've stuck my neck out
because I recollect a man name of Mitchell Curtin,
one of the best bronc-busters in the country, about
five years ago.'

He paused and locked gazes with Dawson – whose
face was interested, but otherwise without expression.

'Yeah,' Dawson said after some moments, very sober
now. 'I knew him. He was a field medic in the same
corps as me. Like you said, best bronc-buster around –
till he got drunk and some of his pards threw him into
an empty box car. Figured it'd be a good joke; he'd
wonder where the hell he was when he woke.'

'I heard them bronco boys played rough.'

'Yeah. Made a bad mistake. Picked a train patrolled
by Deadwood. Railroad said he got hurt when he *fell*
off the train but we knew better. Mitch can't get

around without crutches now. Wife works as a book-keeper in some lousy store in a two-man-and-a-dog town, fightin' off the local Romeos. He earns a few bucks telling tales about his bronc-bustin' days in a saloon. A lousy life for them – and their little gal.'

He sounded sadly wistful, and Britt frowned, spoke quietly, 'Helluva come-down. You wouldn't've been one of them . . . "pards" who put him in that box car, would you?'

Dawson's gaze was steady. 'Might've been.'

After a long moment, the lawman nodded slightly. 'Well, I'd say Deadwood got his come-uppance tonight. Deserved it, too – every last broken bone.'

Dawson breathed a sigh as Britt left and slipped the leather thong that was the door latch over the nail head there for that purpose.

He had taken a chance with Britt and was mighty lucky not to be headed for the local chain gang.

But he knew he had better not try it again. . . .

He was eating breakfast in a diner when a shadow fell across his plate of bacon and eggs. It was Doc Fallon, carrying a cup of coffee.

'Mind if I join you?'

'Help yourself, Doc.'

Dawson ate, Fallon sipped his coffee, watching. Matt started to feel uncomfortable. 'Somethin'. . . ?'

'I was just thinking that whoever worked over Deadwood must be a vengeful man.' Dawson grunted and chewed some more bacon rind. 'Or squaring a grudge for someone unable to do it himself. Maybe you're wondering why Marshal Britt isn't making any great fuss about finding out who it was?'

'Nope.' It didn't sound too convincing.

Fallon smiled thinly. 'You're luckier than you know. Lyndon had a son, fought in the War. Mighty proud of him. Wounded in the Cross Keys Landing massacre. The patrol had to retreat but couldn't take their wounded with them. There was a field medic, never identified, who refused to leave Britt's son, who was dying in terrible pain. He died in the medic's arms just before the Yankees bayoneted the medic himself. He'd given what comfort he could to Britt's son even though it cost him his own life.' Fallon set down his cup and took a cheroot from a leather folder, offered one to Dawson. When they were burning, Fallon continued: 'So Britt's always had a soft spot for field medics ever since.'

Dawson showed his surprise. 'That's why he's given me a break, because I'd been a field medic?'

Fallon nodded. 'I wouldn't even whisper that in his hearing. It might give someone the idea that Lyndon Britt was halfway human beneath that tough exterior he likes to show.'

Dawson spoke slowly. 'Wondered why. He must've guessed was me beat up Deadwood. I don't regret what I done, Doc.'

'No. I'd say you must feel a good deal of relief, now you've had a chance to ease your conscience some over that "joke" that backfired so badly all those years ago.'

Dawson set down knife and fork, picked up his

cheroot and took a drag. 'You're a smart old man, Doc. Don't reckon I'll ever feel easy about that foolishness, though.'

'To your credit. But young men painting a town red don't always think, or act very responsibly, Mr Dawson. I believe you did a fine job on Deadwood. You hit the best parts of the human body to cripple a brute like that.'

'What'll happen to him, Doc?'

'I'll send him to a proper hospital in one of the bigger towns down the line. It'll be a long time before he's discharged. I believe he'll need to change his . . . occupation when he is.'

Dawson suddenly smiled and held out his hand, gripping with the medic. 'Thanks, Doc. You're the bearer of good news all round.'

'Just don't push your luck any more. The marshal's made his decision and it's done. It wouldn't have been easy for him.' He paused as if deciding whether to continue. 'He wasn't always like this, you know. He used to be very, very hard, a by-the-book man, no compromise to friend or foe. Then he had a heart attack. As often happens, it gave him a new perspective on life. In his early years he was all fists and guns and boots; you broke the law, you paid for it. No comebacks. Now he's doing his best to set some sort of balance. Still following the spirit of the law, but interpreting it according to the situation. Know what I mean? Some things he'd have thrown a man in jail for without thought years ago. Now he tends to take a more . . . liberal view. Not *lenient*, no! There'll be some penalty but not necessarily as harsh as he used to make it. He's realized human beings are fraught with foibles, specially after booze.'

'Not goin' soft! Not Lyndon Britt!'

'Hush your mouth, Matt Dawson! Just be grateful, and careful. And forget we ever had this conversation.'

'I don't recollect havin' any sort of conversation with you, Doc. How's work in these parts?'

Fallon studied him briefly. 'If you're a cowhand, the ranches out in the valley across the river are mighty . . . busy, right now. I've heard they're hiring. Try Box K. Or' – he paused briefly – 'or even Rocking R.'

Dawson nodded gently, frowning slightly as he murmured. 'Thanks, I'll give 'em a try.'

But he wondered why the medic had paused before saying 'busy'?

Somehow it had seemed kind of . . . ominous.

CHAPTER 4

HIRED HAND

They were waiting for him in the livery.

He should have figured something was out of kilter when the shifty-eyed hostler told him he had moved his horse.

'The boy put him in the wrong stall earlier,' he said, a lean, rawboned man in bib-and-brace overalls and with a well-chewed cigar-stub angled out of a corner of his mouth. 'That one's reserved, so I had your dun put down the end there, right along near the rear door. You see where I mean?'

'Might if I had a telescope,' Dawson said, frowning.

'Aw, yeah, well I had to leave the big door swung inwards today so we can fix a loose hinge. It does sorta cut the light. I'll guide you down if you want.'

'Forget it. If I come back, I'll expect a stall nearer the front.'

'Sure, no problem. Just that there's a bunch of

Rocking R riders in for a couple days. Have to give locals preference you know.'

'I've heard of it happening,' Dawson said making his way towards the rear of the stables.

He had to pass the office, where the livery man had propped up a couple of pieces of broken mirror so he could see anyone who entered, front or rear, when he was at his desk. Matt glanced up incuriously as he went by, and almost faltered, but kept the pace going.

Something moved back there, indistinct in the shadowed area where the dun was supposed to be. And it wasn't a horse.

He kept walking, trying to act relaxed and not suspicious, but he let his right hand trail close to the butt of his six-gun as he saw the movement in the stall itself, alongside the dun. So he stepped to the side and eased along the front of the other stalls. All were empty and he realized too late that the man moving around with the dun was a decoy, just to hold his attention.

Two of them came out of the other darkened stalls, one from each side. He was no gunfighter but his Colt started to lift at a reasonable speed, and one of the attackers yelled.

'Watch it, Spud!'

Then one of them tackled him around the hips, the impact driving him towards the second man. The third one rushed out of the stall, swinging a coiled bridle. It whistled and Dawson grunted as a buckle bit into his shoulder. He ducked on that side, bending down quickly, but he was still being carried forward by the tackler.

40

He slammed into the partition post, breath gusting out of him, his head taking a glancing blow that nonetheless showered streaking stars across his vision. The bridle came back towards him and he ducked fast enough for it to knock his hat off, then pass on to take one of the others in the face. The man screamed and, still dazed, Dawson went for him; nothing like a yelling, hurt man to grab the attention of his fellow-attackers.

Matt drove a fist into the bleeding face, kicked him in the shins. The man doubled over with a guttural sound, and Dawson thudded an elbow into the back of his head before a set of hard knuckles slammed into his neck like a cleaver into a side of beef. He floundered several feet, grasping at anything that would keep him from going down. But the one with the bridle caught him across the wounded side and he fell to one knee. A fist like a hammer took him on the side of the head. He crashed against the wall, still on one knee.

Then they started with the boots, thudding into him as he tried to cover his head with his arms. He wrenched away and a boot hooked his shoulder, flattening him into a corner. He quickly dropped back on his shoulders and kicked up, both legs going. He caught a man stepping in squarely in the belly. The man moaned sickly, grasped himself and kind of weaved on to his knees, snivelling as he fought for breath.

Dawson rolled and kicked him in the chest, knocking him into one of the others who was starting to

41

close in. The man instinctively grabbed at his hurt pard and Dawson spun away towards the third one.

This man had the bridle raised for the heaviest blow yet and Dawson rolled into the stall, under the dun which snorted and stomped. He was lucky he didn't catch a hoof in the head, but he came to his feet on the far side of the horse. He slapped the reins loose from the feed bin and thrust against the dun with all his strength.

Snorting and wrenching its head side to side, it surged into the two bloody men trying to get at him. One yelled and went down under the dun's belly, intent only on protecting himself from those stomping hoofs. The other man jumped back and the horse charged past, knocking him violently against a post and continued on down the aisle. The startled livery man tried to stop him.

Gasping, hurt, Dawson staggered out of the stall and saw the man with the hurt belly leaning against a partition, bringing up a gun, shakily. The remaining man went for his six-gun, too. That left Matt Dawson no choice.

He dived for the ground inside the stall, where his own gun had fallen and lay half-covered by straw. The other guns blasted, expecting him to be on his feet. He rolled, snatched up the Colt as he went and thrust up to his knees, the gun blazing three fast shots as he chopped at the bent hammer spur. Splinters flew and both men went down, one heavily and limp, the other crashing on to his side, sobbing pain as he grabbed a shattered arm.

By the time Dawson was breathing normally again it seemed like half the town had crowded into the livery. Then Marshal Britt pushed his way through, holding a sawn-off shotgun.

He looked at the bloody scene and the man who had not gone for his gun, then to Dawson, who still held his Colt, just a wisp of smoke still curling from the muzzle.

'That one not movin' – he dead?' Britt asked and the livery man, licking his lips and looking at Dawson, nodded.

'This feller nailed 'em clean as you like. They started the shootin', though.'

Britt's dark eyes bored into the hostler. 'How'd it get going?'

The stable man shifted uncomfortably from foot to foot. 'Aw – well, Jingo' – he gestured to the dead man – 'an' Spud an' Rudy told me to move the dun to one of the back stalls. They stayed in the shadows and when I sent Dawson down – they – jumped him.'

'That right, Dawson?'

Matt nodded.

'What'd they want?'

'Didn't say. Just started in beatin' me up.'

Britt walked across to the man who was still holding his belly, low down, sprawled in a corner, sweating. Britt kicked him none too gently in the side. 'What you got to say, Spud?'

'Aw. We heard how he – brung Luke Rafter in – with all his pockets turned out. Robbin' the dead ain't anythin' we figure we gotta stand for—'

43

Dawson snapped his head up, gave the man a hot glare, then shifted his gaze to the marshal. 'They sure look like high-moral cowpunchers, don't they? Or do I mean yellow livered coyotes?'

'Now you listen—' started the hurt man, but Britt kicked him in the side again.

'Shut up, Spud. You and Rudy and Jingo have been rollin' drunks and beatin' up on folk for a long time. I've had you all in jail, an' last time I told you if I had to arrest any of you again, you were goin' straight to the chain gang.'

Spud looked alarmed, shot the wounded Rudy a wild look.

Rudy licked his bleeding lips. 'Aw, look, Marshal, we just done what we was told. Lafe said go in an' straighten out this Dawson *hombre*, find out what he took from Luke Rafter. Lafe's the boss, Marshal—'

'And I'll be asking him why he set you dumb bastards on Dawson. Get up and lean your hands on the wall, spread your legs and stay there till I tell you otherwise.'

They wanted to give him an argument but when he cocked the shotgun hammers they obeyed quickly enough. Then Britt looked hard at Dawson who was mopping blood from his face.

'You never got anythin' from Luke's pockets, did you?' At Dawson's shake of his head, he added, 'How about the saddle-bags?'

'I was only interested in grub but there wasn't any, just a couple shirts and spare socks, which I kept.'

'Uh-huh.' Britt kept staring hard, ignoring the

44

moans from the men leaning on the stall. 'You know, Dawson, I think it's time you quit my town for keeps. Ever since you rode in I seem to've been counting the dead and maimed. Now you get cleaned up, ride out – and stay out.'

Matt Dawson didn't give him any argument.

'I don't care to hire a man who's obviously just been in a drunken brawl. Good day to you, Mr Dawson.'

'Wait up, ma'am! I was jumped by three fellers in the livery. There was no drunken brawl.'

She paused, a tallish woman, slim with the kind of slimness that comes from constant hard work, her brown hair spilling to her shoulders. Blue eyes regarded him without expression, but it was obvious she was looking at him more closely than a few minutes ago when he'd ridden in on the dun and asked for work. She tilted her small chin but the full lips didn't soften any.

'Being "jumped" by three men doesn't sound as if it was some random thing; there must've been a reason.' He hesitated, then nodded slightly, but before he could speak she suddenly said: 'Oh, so you're that Dawson! The man who brought in Luke Rafter's body!' She was obviously more interested now. 'Did that have anything to do with these three men beating you up?'

'I dunno why you'd think so right away, but they were interested to know what I found on Rafter's body.' He frowned slightly as she stiffened. 'Nothing but his spare shirt,' he tugged at the blue shirt he was wearing, 'and some socks. Not my habit to search dead men, ma'am, and, in any case, someone had already turned his pockets inside out.'

'Do you . . . know who these men were – the ones in the stables, I mean?'

'Jingo, Spud and Rudy I heard them called. Seem to work for someone named Lafe.'

'Lafe Randall. My neighbour. You may've noticed that big sprawling ranch on the slopes, far side of this basin.'

He had and had considered going there to look for work, but this Box K spread, half the size, happened to be closer.

She was studying him even more intently now. 'You have some obvious injuries and you move stiffly. Can I ask what happened to Rocking R's men?'

His gaze was steady. 'Spud and Rudy look no worse than me, but Jingo's dead.' She jumped a little, her lips opening slightly. 'He went for his gun and I shot him.'

He heard her long, deep breath and her bosom swelled against her checked shirt as she dragged it down. 'You're a – gunfighter then?'

'No, ma'am,' he told her tiredly. 'I'm a drifter. I've worked in mines, building dams, laying railroad track, driven cattle, hunted mustangs and mavericks, built log cabins and clapboard barns. You might get the idea by now I'm an all-rounder.'

'Who'll take any job for a dollar?' She spoke stiffly and he smiled thinly.

'I don't hire out my gun, if that's what you're

thinkin'. Told you, I'm no gunfighter. Sure, I've been caught up in range wars, but I don't buy into 'em knowingly.'

'And you say Marshal Britt suggested you try Box K for work?'

'No, it was Doc Fallon.'

She raised her neat eyebrows. 'The good doctor of Durham! Well, perhaps after all, I can use a man of your varied talents, Mr Dawson – Matt, is it?' He nodded, waiting. 'There are no range wars here – as such. But I have to tell you, Lafe Randall and I don't get along.'

He waited for her to say why but she offered no explanation, which was fair enough. 'I can only pay the usual forty and found. I'm a fair cook and I believe in seeing my crew are fed well.' She gave him a quick smile and for that brief moment her face lit up, showing perhaps the real Eadie Kern behind the sober ranch woman. 'I like them to be fit for the amount of work I need doing here.'

'I've never been afraid of hard work, ma'am, and I'll be glad to take you up on your offer.'

'You have no trouble taking orders from a woman?'

He smiled with his split lips and it, too, softened his rugged, battered features briefly. 'Never have, so far.'

'All right. Come down to the bunkhouse and meet the rest of my crew. There are only three others.'

Leading the dun and walking beside Matt, she said, 'I bought out Luke Rafter. I believe he was carrying over three thousand dollars when he left here.'

'Kind of risky, toting that kind of money.'

'He was in a hurry. But you can see why some people are interested to know who shot him – and what they found when they searched him.'

'*Took*, you mean. . . ?'

She nodded gently. 'Yes, *stole* is what I meant, I suppose. Are you – financial, Matt?'

He smiled wryly. 'Got about five bucks and some cents. Marshal lent it to me.' She arched her eyebrows at that. 'I'll pay him back out of my first wages.'

'Indeed.' There was surprise and a touch of respect in the way she said it. 'You and Marshal Britt must get along pretty well.'

'That must be why he told me to ride out and stay out.'

The three ranch hands were just finishing lunch, sitting in the brushwood shade of a ramada attached to the bunkhouse. They watched Dawson closely, all three, as Eadie Kern introduced them.

Curly Knox was young and lived up to his name, a thick mat of curly dark hair edging on to his unlined forehead and sprouting over his ears. He nodded with a quick grin on his boyish face, revealing one broken tooth.

Spanish was swarthy, about Dawson's age, sported a thin moustache above purplish lips and had dark, flashing eyes. Obviously he came from Spanish stock. He nodded politely and said, '*Bienvenida, señor.*'

'*Gracias, amigo*,' Dawson returned.

'From the Border?' asked the third man, Alec Crewe, a man in his early forties, with sprinkles of grey in his bluish-black hair. He had a rugged jaw and traces of a hare-lip but there was little of it in his speech.

'Been there – south of the Rio, too.'

Crewe nodded, looking at Dawson's Colt in the worn holster. 'You have that look.' He half-rose from the bench, offering a calloused hand. 'Glad to know you. I'm sort of the foreman here, though Eadie really gives the orders.'

Setting things straight right from the start.

'Have yourself some food, Matt, then go with Spanish. He's stringing fences around our north pasture.'

Dawson looked at her quickly. 'I saw a buckboard under a tree when I rode in. Looked like bales of barbed wire in the back.'

'You have something against barbed wire?' She was immediately on the defensive.

Matt hesitated, then shrugged. 'No more than any man who's worked cattle, I guess. Prefer to do without it.'

'When you have a spread of your own – if ever – you can make that decision, Matt.'

Put in his place, he nodded, 'Sure. Could I get some vittles? Must be the fresh air's sharpened my appetite.'

'There is some cornpone and a few strips of sow-belly left,' volunteered Spanish, standing now and showing himself to be taller than Dawson had thought. 'I'll show you – but they'll be mostly cold.'

'I could eat a bobcat raw right now.'

Dawson's words brought a faint smile to their faces and he followed Spanish into the bunkhouse.

'You hired yourself a troubleshooter?' Crewe asked the girl, and her eyes narrowed.

'I've hired a man to take Luke's place, Alec. Some of Randall's men attacked him in town. It seemed like a good idea to have someone on the payroll who already has a grudge against Rocking R.'

Crewe pursed his lips. 'Makes sense, I guess.'

'Does to me,' offered Curly as if anyone was interested in what he thought. But it didn't bother him; he took out a battered harmonica and played a few bars of *Turkey in the Straw* before Eadie told him to settle down and finish digging the irrigation ditch from the creek to the vegetable garden behind the main house.

Curly moved off, whistling, and Alec Crewe said, 'That ain't really cowhand's work, Eadie.'

'It's work I want done. Just as I want you to bring that bunch of heifers in to the north pasture when Spanish and Dawson finish the fence.'

There was challenge in her words and a line of small muscles bunched along his jaw, but he nodded jerkily.

'You're the boss.'

'Try to remember that, Alec. I'm riding into town to arrange Luke's funeral. I think I owe him that much.'

'I'd say so,' Crewe agreed in clipped tones as he jammed his curlbrim hat on his head, then feigned not to notice the narrowing of her eyes as she watched him walk towards the corrals.

Well, she had a full crew again – and Matt Dawson

just might be the man she needed to stand up against Lafe Randall and his hardcases.

CHAPTER 5

THE MAP

Lafe Randall was a fine-looking man: early thirties, broad shouldered, slim-hipped, and handsome with a strong jaw and a steady, unsettling stare out of ice-blue eyes. He also had a ready smile for the ladies – or anyone he figured could do him a favour or help him get what he wanted at that particular time.

He dressed neatly, not flashy, but his clothes were always clean and fitted well, as they should. He had them hand-made in Denver by descendants of Dutch tailors, the cloth being mostly imported.

Lafe had a pleasant voice and most folk, on first meeting him, or even during the first *few* meetings, figured here was a fine man, a prosperous rancher, a credit to his profession, the culture of the Western cattleman.

But Lafe Randall was an unmitigated bastard.

His looks got him by in most places; his manners

could be turned on and off, and that smile set the female cardiac organs – and maybe some other parts of their anatomy – all aflutter.

But it was an act. Randall had got where he was by underhand, double-crossing deals, fast – and smooth – talking and a ruthlessness that could have been inherited from Genghis Khan. He had a habit of moving into an area, using all his charm to get what he wanted at whatever the cost, both in money and human misery, before showing his true colours. Then he made a clean sweep, left financial and physical ruin in his wake, and moved on to enjoy the spoils and plan his next coup. He had used so many names that he could barely recollect his given one, which in no way resembled 'Lafe Randall'.

His way of life inevitably left blood on his hands but that worried him no more than the temporary stain of spilled coffee.

So when he rode into Box K's front yard, with his hardcase bodyguard, Link Hauser, Eadie Kern gave him no more than a barely civil 'howdy', as she sat on her porch at a small round table where there were notebooks and papers.

'Hear you've hired yourself a gunfighter.'

'If you want to listen to stupid gossip that's your affair, Lafe. But I'm not surprised if you take it as genuine.'

His sunny smile closed in a little at the edges and his eyes seemed more icy than usual. 'Always niggling, Eadie. Don't know why you bother. You can't get a rise out of me. Thought you'd've realized that long ago.'

She hipped around a little in her chair. 'Lafe, I realized a lot of things about you long ago; in fact, almost as soon as you moved into this neck of the woods. I've met your kind before.'

'But have you managed to handle "my kind"?'

'If I can do it without getting my own hands dirty, I'll give it a try.'

The smile vanished. 'All right, Eadie! If that's the way you want it.'

He gestured to the silent rider with him. Link Hauser was only medium tall, overweight, with a belly that stretched his trouser belt to the last buckle notch. Not so the wide, hand-tooled gunbelt: that had been made specially for him in El Paso; it fitted snug and comfortable at all times, easily supporting his two big stag-handled Colts.

'Link's heard of this Matt Dawson. Rough and tough, with a few kills under his belt. Aw, not a man who goes looking for gun trouble, but one who can handle it if it comes his way. I guess if you pay him enough it'll go whichever way you want it to and he'll see to it.'

'He's no gunfighter.'

Link chuckled. 'I'd bet on that!' His voice was too thin for his body but he looked genuinely amused.

Eadie tried not to seem too worried. 'He's an experienced cowhand and that's why I hired him.'

'Oh? Not because he killed Jingo, winged Rudy, crippled that railroad thug who calls himself Deadwood?'

'No, not for any of those reasons. So don't go

reading any more into this than there is, Lafe. Lyndon Britt might have something to say about it if you were to use it as an excuse to bring in some fast guns of your own.'

'He already has one!' Link said stiffly, adding: 'Don't worry none about Britt. That ol' hasbeen's just too plumb lazy to lie down an' die. Might have to help him along, sometime.'

Eadie's face reflected her alarm briefly, but Randall saw it and smiled faintly, still looking handsome and friendly.

'It's your business who you hire, of course, Eadie – as it's mine who I choose to put on my payroll. Just thought I'd check in with you.' He started to wheel his big sorrel with its concha-studded saddle and bridle, paused and winked. 'Have to say, you haven't convinced me this Dawson's not a gunfighter you sent for.'

Eadie stood, trying to control her rising anger. She gathered her papers with jerky motions, her arms holding the pile awkwardly. 'I don't really care what you believe, Lafe. But I will say this: if I were you, I wouldn't try to rawhide Matt Dawson. Whatever he is, he has a short fuse – and a long memory. You know the way out. Don't lose time using it.'

She started to move towards the house door and some of the papers spilled from her grasp, one floating down off the porch. Randall was quick to nod at Link Hauser; and the gunfighter moved surprisingly fast and not without grace as he dismounted and scooped it up. Randall clicked his fingers and Link handed it to him.

'Give me that!' Eadie snapped. 'It belongs to me!'

Lafe left Hauser to block her at the steps while he unfolded the large sheet of paper.

It was a hand-drawn map of the original Spanish Grant in this basin, very decorative in the style of the old Madrid cartographers but not very accurate, which didn't seem to matter in the 1700s or early 1800s. The prettier, the better. . . .

Hauser grinned and stepped this way and that, blocking Eadie's attempts to get off the short set of steps and reach the map, which Randall was studying.

The rancher glanced up, and for a moment his handsome face was tight and ugly – but only for a moment.

'So, you've got your hands on a copy of the original map, eh? Lacks detail. Only the perimeters of the Grant are shown. No accurate measurements within the area where the land was broken up into packages. Mmmmm, I can see where Rocking R'd be, but if it shows this river or creek's where it really is. . . .' He looked up and smiled at the angry girl. 'Why, it just could be that one of our boundaries is out by quite a few yards. Taking a guess, I'd say it's yours, Eadie, and you're encroaching on my land. Tut-tut!'

Then he crumpled the map, threw it to the ground and nodded to Hauser, who released the girl he had been holding against the bottom stair post. She ran to pick up the map before it could blow away and Randall was laughing as he and Hauser mounted and rode away, throwing over his shoulder, 'Think I better see my lawyer about this.'

Eadie Kern looked mighty worried as she smoothed out the thick, crumpled paper.

What if Lafe Randall was right about the position of her boundary all along?

It didn't bear thinking about, because, if that were so, she could be ruined.

After supper, limbs aching and fingers, thumbs and hands with various pricks and cuts from the wire barbs, Dawson tried to roll a cigarette, but the motion set his minor wounds bleeding and the blood ruined the paper. Eadie took pity on him and, smiling, relieved him of his slim sack of tobacco and wheat straw papers and deftly rolled him a cigarette. While he smoked it, she made up four more.

'That ought to see you through until morning.'

He nodded, exhaling smoke. 'Thanks. You make a pretty good quirley.'

'My father taught me when he felt arthritis beginning to cripple his hands.' She seemed pensive briefly, then said, 'Lafe Randall visited me today. He's making out you're a gunfighter. I believe it's merely an excuse so he can bring in a couple of his own.'

The whole crew was sitting outside the bunkhouse on the bench seat below the *ramada*, enjoying the cool of evening. Curly snapped his head up, looking worried.

'Hey! That sounds like – like there's gonna be a range war!'

'I don't think so, Curly,' she told him quietly, though she looked a little worried. 'I won't let it go that far. I'm sure Marshal Britt will back me up.'

She looked at Spanish and Crewe; the latter said, 'One time he would've, without hesitation. But he's a mite more ... cautious these days since his heart attack.'

'Lyndon Britt will do what is right,' Spanish said flatly.

'Maybe I ought to move on before it gets to the stage where Randall brings in some fast gun,' Dawson said.

He was surprised – pleasantly so – when Eadie reached out and placed a hand on his forearm. 'There's no need for that, Matt. But Lafe has given me some worry – Spanish has a brother who works for the Mexican government in Mexico City. He's managed to get me a copy of the original Spanish Grant in Durham Bend, when this part of Texas belonged to Mexico.' She took the crumpled map out of an apron pocket and spread it out across her knees. 'Randall saw it, says my boundary is misplaced several yards into his land.'

'How could he tell?' Dawson asked. 'Look at all these sketches – cherubs blowing clouds, waterholes or lakes – *lagos*, mountains that look like volcanoes, buffalo skulls – and, my God, they must've been giant-size! There's no scale or correct proportions. The map doesn't tell you much – just shows a general area and lots of decoration.'

'That's how maps were made when this one was first drawn.'

'Yeah. I've seen old maps like it before. But how can

Randall pick out any borders of the present land distribution? Here's something marked *D'oro* and even a mine entrance sketched in. This is no guide, Eadie.'

She gave him a silent sober look, then reached out and took the map from him, folding it up again. She sighed.

'You're right. It was stupid of me to think this could be used to re-size Box K. It'd be just like Lafe Randall to pull a stunt, claiming the boundaries are wrong and—' She stopped abruptly.

Coming in on the cool air of early evening was a ragged volley of distant shots, with the barely heard bawling of cattle mixed in.

'Judas priest!' Crewe jumped to his feet. 'That's coming from the north pasture, where we just threw up the new fences!'

'And moved in a herd of nigh on a hundred steers not three hours ago!' added Spanish, jumping up also, perturbed.

Dawson was already hurrying towards the corrals. 'Curly,' he said, 'you stay with Eadie!'

'I'm not staying here!' called the girl running back into the house.

Dawson didn't answer as he and Spanish ducked through the corral fence, selecting their mounts. Curly stood uncertainly until Eadie came out holding a rifle.

'Come on, Curly! Move!' she snapped, and minutes later all five of them galloped out into the darkening night.

The clatter of their racing mounts drowned out any

59

more gunfire and all except a couple of lone bellows from the steers.

Matt Dawson unsheathed his own rifle from the saddle scabbard, and levered a cartridge into the breech, carrying the weapon in one hand.

He figured he would need this before many more minutes had gone by.

CHAPTER 6

STAMPEDE

They topped the slope and the early-rising moon threw enough light to show them the pall of dust lifted by the stampeding steers, with a glimpse or two of riders down there hazing them along. One man triggered two shots into the air and Dawson threw his rifle to his shoulder, straightened in the saddle and gripped the running dun firmly with his legs.

He fired, levered, fired again. The ranny down there started to swing wildly aside but the second bullet found his mount and knocked it sideways, whickering wildly. The man fought it desperately, trying to stay seated, and managed to get the horse running again, though it was with an uneven stride and the animal veered away from the tail of the herd.

Spanish's carbine cracked like a whip in the hands of a madman: at least five rapid shots. Dawson saw a rider trying to clear the trampled barbed wire of the fence punched from the saddle. He hit the wire and his thrashing entangled him in the strands immediately.

He started to scream as the barbs slashed through his clothes and sliced his flesh.

Matt veered, the dun clearing the trampled wire area. He saw the snapped-off posts and, even at this speed and in this fast-fading light, he saw tufts of hair caught on the gleaming barbs of the strands.

The herd had crashed through in their terror; he wondered how many they would find torn up and bleeding when that dust cloud cleared. There was a crash and a yell and he whipped round in the saddle in time to see the horse he had wounded going down. It weaved drunkenly and its legs folded. The rider screamed curses, raked the already suffering animal with his spurs. When it continued to fall he leapt from the saddle, sprawled and rolled to his feet.

He turned and ran towards the creek that gleamed a quarter of a mile distant and where a couple of other riders were veering away from the terrified steers. He palmed up his six-gun, fired wildly under his arm at Dawson.

Matt reined the dun aside, then spurred forward as the panicked man spun and started running. Dawson rode him down ruthlessly, feeling the solid jar as the flying dun's chest crashed into him. The man's body was hurled a good six feet. He skidded through the dirt, then started to get up groggily.

Dawson leaned from the saddle as he rode by and slammed his rifle butt across his head. The hat flew off and hair swirled around the man's contorted face as he collapsed. Without glancing at him, Dawson rode on towards the herd and the rider still hazed it on, shooting into the air, yelling, keeping up the terror.

Then he saw why.

The creek was low here: a stretch of gluey mud five yards wide between the muddy water and solid ground.

'Stop them!'

He just managed to hear Eadie's frantic call, and he swerved to do what he could. Spanish and Alec Crewe were closer and they slammed in from one side, right at the edge of the mud, shooting into the front line of the herd. He saw three steers go down, those behind thundering on relentlessly, trampling the downed beasts, some falling over them and bellowing before they too were trampled.

It was the only way to stop the main bunch: slaughter the front line, use it as a barrier, even if some other steers were hurt or killed, but it would keep the main body of cattle out of the mud.

Even as he watched, reloading his hot rifle, he saw the herd breaking up, veering to the side. The din of animals in torment and terror was deafening. Curly and Eadie rode in and actually turned a handful of steers back towards Box K. Alec and Spanish found themselves trapped as steers crashed around them. They lifted their mounts up, pawing the air, whickering, rolling-eyed. It served to frighten the already terrified animals and they veered away as Dawson rode in and fired his six-gun into the ground in front of the steers' forefeet. He emptied the gun, saw the line was breaking more, now beginning to scatter into small groups and a few loners.

The stampede was over, slowing now, lots of bawling and an occasional bellow could be heard as horns ripped hot flesh beneath dusty hides. But the thunder of fear-driven hoofs had faded to nothing.

And they were clear of the mud flats, no more than seven or eight of the animals having floundered in, unable to stop in time. Dawson and Spanish rescued four with their ropes but the others were stuck fast and sinking. Crewe dispatched them with a single shot each from his rifle.

Eadie, breathless, hair all awry because she was also hatless, face layered with dirt and leaves and a few spots of blood, looked at the mess as intermittent bellowing tore through the half-light. *My God! What a mess!* she thought. *Twenty steers lost, a handful that'll have to be destroyed and— But, wait! I could've lost everything!*

Abruptly, she worked up a smile as she faced her men.

'Best – damn crew this – side of the – Rio!' she gasped. 'Let's dismount while they – settle down – we've earned a rest.' She lifted her voice suddenly, as Dawson turned his blowing dun. 'Where're you going, Matt?'

'To find that ranny I knocked out, and the one caught in the barbed wire. Don't you want to know who did this to you?'

Damn right she did! She nodded and said, 'And *why*!'

But they were disappointed.

The man Dawson had shot the horse from under had apparently been trampled by a bunch of the stampeding steers; he was not pretty to look at and Spanish stripped the saddle blanket off the man's dead horse and draped it over him.

The one who had become tangled in the barbed wire with his panic-driven thrashings had writhed and thrown himself around so much that the barbs had cut him to pieces; there must have been a hundred cuts on his body, but only one really counted: the long, deep gash in the left side of his neck, that had punctured the carotid artery.

The raider had bled to death.

'Know either of them?' Dawson asked Eadie and the others quietly, but they shook their heads and Eadie, white-faced walked away, not looking at the dead men.

'Strangers round here,' Crewe said.

'Where's Curly?' Eadie suddenly asked, a slight alarm in her tone. 'I thought he went down to the mudline.'

'He rode up to the ford,' Spanish told her. 'I think he went after that lone rider who headed that way.'

'But Curly's never done anything like that before!' She turned towards Dawson. 'He's just a kid! A good cowboy but he's no manhunter.'

Matt knew she was asking him to go after Curly. He nodded without speaking, mounted the dun, who was just settling down to normal breathing and investigating a small patch of juicy grass. It gave a snort of displeasure but responded to the reins and his heels touching the hot flanks.

He rode out fast, along the creek, the water gleaming like hammered silver in the now high moon's light.

'Maybe I better. . . .' started Alec Crewe, gesturing towards Dawson.

'He don't need help,' Spanish said gruffly. 'Not that one. He'll never need help in such a chore.'

It seemed like only a few minutes after Spanish spoke that they heard the first gunshots.

Curly had either pinned down the escaping raider, or the man had lain in wait and ambushed him.

Dawson urged the dun on, straining to see as the shadow of the mountain cut the light here.

The shots crashed over to his left, in a patch of deeper darkness. The kid would probably have ridden straight in if the raider had been cunning enough to make some sound or left some sign to entice him.

It was a death trap and only someone as inexperienced as Curly Knox would have fallen for it.

Dawson kept the dun running and when he came to a patch of soft sand dropped out of the saddle, tightening his grip on the rifle. He had the breath slammed from him and rolled, scrabbling quickly to get behind a line of low rocks.

There was a rattle of gunfire and he managed to pinpoint it as coming from a narrow arroyo. *Kid, if you survive this, you better change your name to 'Lucky'.*

Crouching, he went into the arroyo, shoulders scraping loose dirt from one wall. He froze, cursing the small stones that clattered down. There was a momentary pause in the shooting, then he heard a single, powerful-sounding shot before he heard Curly open up again – leastways, he took it to be Curly as the sounds came from just ahead, closer than the others.

He paused suddenly. *What others?*

The shooting coming from the low rim of the arroyo had stopped. Maybe Curly had had some luck after all and nailed the raider.

Then he heard racing hoofbeats beyond the rim. Puzzled, he took a chance, heaved himself over a bank and threw himself behind a rock. He raised his head cautiously, eyes looking up. There were patches of moonlight and he glimpsed a rider between two rocks, going fast.

Maybe Curly hadn't been so lucky at all – maybe that was why he had stopped shooting.

Movement below caught his attention and he saw the kid standing up, looking around. *Jesus!*

'Curly! Stay down, you blamed idiot!'

Curly crouched quickly, looking about him. 'That you, Matt?'

'Yeah,' Dawson answered curtly and started climbing down. He skidded the last couple of feet and almost fell. 'Hell's teeth, kid, you want to get your head blown off! He was on the run but if he hipped in the saddle and saw you making a good target of yourself standing tall against the pale rock—'

'But that wasn't him.'

'What?'

Curly gestured to a bank a few feet above where they stood. Dawson gripped his rifle tighter as he saw a man's arm dangling there. Lower down he saw the rifle where it had fallen from the owner's grip.

'What the hell. . . ?'

'Someone shot him.'

'You mean, *you* shot him.'

'No, it wasn't me. I had to reload and I was just leverin' a shell into the breech when there was this big booming shot, and I seen this feller stagger, half upright, then fall, one arm hangin' as his gun slid down the bank.' He waved towards the dark line of the higher rim. 'Someone from up there nailed him. I heard him ridin' away.'

Puzzled, Dawson nodded slowly. 'Caught a glimpse of him, thought it was the feller you were after. Might've been a paint he was forking. . . ?' He looked quizzically at Curly.

'Only paint I know of hereabouts, 'cept for a couple of Indians, belongs to Link Hauser.'

By now they had climbed up to where the dead raider lay.

He had been killed by a single shot in the back, the bullet smashing his spine.

'Someone wanted to make sure he didn't do any talkin',' opined Alec Crewe when Dawson and Curly had ridden back to Box K, bringing the dead raider with them.

Eadie looked at Alec sharply. 'What? What are you saying?'

'Just said it. Someone wanted to make sure he didn't talk. So they shot him in the back.'

'Like Luke Rafter,' opined Dawson, and they both looked at him sharply.

'I don't like the implications of all this,' said Eadie Kern slowly. 'Anyway, I've sent Spanish into town to fetch the marshal. Does anyone know him?'

She hadn't looked at the dead man's face and steeled herself now as Crewe twisted fingers in the straw-coloured hair and yanked the man's head up. Curly held the lantern closer.

No one knew him.

'Another stranger. Three of them ride in, round the barbed wire. . . .' Dawson started and Crew frowned.

'What d'you mean *round* the barbed wire?'

'They followed the creek but didn't cut the wire. They lowered the rails on the pole fence and then drove the cows into and through the barbed wire.'

'That was – cruel!' Eadie said, but obviously puzzled. 'Why would rustlers risk tearing up the steers like that. . . ?'

'I think Matt's sayin' they weren't just rustlers, Eadie.' Crewe spoke quietly, watching Dawson's face.

She too looked sharply at Dawson. 'You think someone merely wanted to stampede my steers *through* the barbed wire, no matter whether they were – torn up by it or not?'

Matt nodded. 'Then run them into the mud strip and let them founder.'

She stared with something like horror, lips parted. 'To – destroy my herd!'

'How hard would that hit you?'

'Well, they were prime steers, Spanish and Alec

69

brought them up from the San Antonio auctions. I – er – wanted Box K to be known for quality beef and I – put a good deal of my money into that herd.'

'In other words, it would hurt you, financially, but wouldn't ruin you?'

She half-smiled, ruefully. 'I still owe money on that herd, and the barbed wire didn't come cheap. I have other debts and obligatons, too. I would find it pretty damn difficult if I didn't have that herd to drive to market. As it is, well, I suppose we'll have to wait until daylight to find out how many steers were lost for certain.'

'There's enough light for a tally,' Crewe said. 'I can do a rough one, startin' now, Eadie. Come lend a hand, Curly.'

They rode off to where the cattle were still settling down, a few random bellows drifting into the night.

Dawson suddenly turned to his horse and slid the rifle out of the saddle scabbard, startling her when he worked the lever. 'Riders comin'!'

She heard them then, coming up the slope from the bottom trail. Dawson grabbed her by the arm and pulled her down beside him at the end of the porch, crouching, rifle at the ready as he moved protectively in front of her and closed the slide over the lantern.

'Can you tell how many?'

'Five or six at a guess. There they are, coming round the barn.'

Three men rode in that way, but four others came sweeping in from behind the corrals. Light gleamed off gun barrels and Matt lifted the rifle, tensed and ready.

'Hello, the house!' a deep voice boomed. 'You all right, Eadie?'

'It's Lafe Randall,' she said and there was relief in her voice as she stood and stepped around Dawson. He rose slowly and stayed in the cover of the porch shadow as she called back to Randall.

'I'm all right, Lafe. What brings you here?'

'Chuck rode in from night-herdin' my south pasture, said there seemed to be a lot of shootin' comin' from over this way, I sent a man to the high slope to see, and he thought he heard bawling cows as well as gunfire. So we come to see if you need any help.'

'Thank you, Lafe, but it's all over now. Three rustlers tried to steal my prime herd by driving it through my new fence.'

'*Through?* You mean the bob-wire fence you just built? That'd be crazy, it'd rip pan-size steaks off the cows!'

'Or mebbe it was so the herd'd trample the fence and destroy it. Two hits in one.'

Randall hipped fast in the saddle as Dawson stepped out into the light, rifle held casually, but finger only an inch from the trigger, and thumb on the hammer spur.

The riders moved restlessly in their saddles and Matt noticed the paint gelding. He looked up at the rider.

'I've seen you before – but a long way from here.'

'Dodge. 'Bout three year ago,' Link Hauser said casually, but there was a hint of harshness in his words.

71

Dawson nodded slowly. 'Rifle shoot, as I recall. You took out the prize. Using a Sharps. Bullet was so heavy it smashed the target. Yeah, I recollect now. Link Hauser, right?'

'Uh-huh,' Hauser admitted quietly. 'And you're Matt Dawson. One of Masterson's deputies. Took on the Ringo Brothers, all three. Killed two, laid up the other one for months, and then you tossed him in jail.'

Eadie looked at Dawson sharply. 'You never mentioned you'd been a lawman.'

'Didn't think it mattered, seein' as you were hiring me to punch cattle.'

'So you're Dawson.' Heads turned and looked at Randall who was leaning on his saddle horn now. 'Hear you're pretty tough, gettin' thrown off trains and so on.'

'Don't bounce too well, so I wouldn't recommend it.'

Randall chuckled, leaned down, hand outstretched. 'Lafe Randall, Eadie's neighbour. You caught up with these rustlers or whatever they were, eh?'

As Dawson shook hands perfunctorily, he said, 'More like raiders. Two died in the pasture, one under the stampede, other tangled in the wire.'

Link Hauser spat. 'Told you that damn bob-wire was deadly! Range is better off without it. Dunno why anyone who didn't want trouble would use it.'

He looked challengingly at Eadie and she said calmly, 'It seemed the best way to keep my herd from breaking through and getting bogged in the mud

72

strip.'

'Yeah, OK in theory, Eadie.' Randall spoke up. 'But see, it did bring you trouble, anyway, from those three rustlers.'

'Don't think they cared about the herd one way or t'other,' Dawson told him flatly. 'They were paid to stampede that herd and bog it down – wipe out the fence at the same time. Keep everyone happy. Except Eadie.'

There was a brief silence, then one of the riders sniffed and spat and another coughed, breaking the tension.

'How you know somethin' like that?' asked Hauser, his scepticism plain.

'We checked the saddle-bags on the two dead mounts and on this hoss.' Dawson nodded towards the patient horse with the dead man. 'All three had money; more than they would've earned as ranch hands, and I dunno of any rustler with three hundred dollars burnin' a hole in his pocket who wouldn't be at some whorehouse or gamblin' saloon, waitin' his turn.'

'Three hundred!' exclaimed Randall.

'In new hundred-dollar bills.'

'New?' Randall echoed, puzzled by Matt's emphasis.

'Yeah. Brand new, crisp as a fresh-baked cracker.' Dawson smiled crookedly. 'Never circulated. But bills that size don't get seen much out here. Mostly in the city, or between banks, or as a special request from a customer.'

Randall moved uneasily: Dawson was getting at something here, but he couldn't figure what.

Until Eadie Kern told him:

'I got some from the bank when I bought out Luke Rafter. In fact, I took almost all of the bank's supply, but, as Matt said, this isn't an area where every man and his dog even knows what a hundred-dollar bill looks like.'

'So?' Randall sounded tight, tried to appear bored, but it was obvious he was pretty tense.

'Luke Rafter wanted cash when I bought his Lazy J. He had some deal going in Oregon and he was taking the three thousand dollars I paid him for his spread with him. The banker tried to talk him out of it, told him a bank draft would be much safer, but Luke was adamant: only cash would do. He said if he took it in hundred-dollar bills it wouldn't be so bulky and would be easier to hide. So the banker paid him in hundred-dollar bills.'

Dawson saw by Randall's face that the rancher was beginning to see what was coming. So he didn't disappoint him.

'It's almost certain sure the bills we found in the saddle-bags of these raiders came from the money Rafter was carrying when he was shot in the back and dragged by his horse. The bank'll have records of their serial numbers, so it'll be easy enough to check out.'

No one said anything, but both horses and men moved restlessly.

'So, looks like whoever paid off these hardcases used Rafter's money, and they had to backshoot him to get it. Marshal Britt's gonna think the same when he gets here.'

Randall stiffened and Hauser swore softly.

'Britt's comin' here?'

'I sent Spanish to fetch him,' Eadie said coolly. 'More dead men and an attempt to rustle my herd. I had no choice but to let the law know. Why, Lafe? Does that upset you in some way?'

Randall glared. 'Not me. But if you got Britt comin', you won't need any help from us.'

He wrenched his horse's head around roughly and jammed in the spurs. Link Hauser and the other Rocking R men rode after him.

Dawson smiled crookedly at Eadie, who looked a little surprised at Randall's sudden departure.

'Thanks anyway, Lafe,' she called belatedly but he made no sign that he had heard: if anything, he and his men increased their pace. 'Seems in a hurry.'

Dawson grinned. 'I think we spooked him.'

CHAPTER 7

DEAD END

Marshal Britt was grumpy when he reached Box K with Spanish – actually, the cowhand rode on ahead and alerted Eadie and the others to the lawman's imminent arrival.

'He don't like ridin' far and his rheumatism's givin' him gyp, so don't expect smiles or gay laughter.'

Eadie nodded, quite serious as she told Dawson, 'Lyndon's getting old and the hard life he's led for so long is starting to catch up with him.'

'He should retire.'

'I believe he's thinking of it. But I also believe he's scared at the same time.'

'Can't imagine Britt bein' scared of anything.'

'An old man, no family. I wouldn't say *no* friends, but – well everyone is more an acquaintnce than a friend, around Durham. Not a happy prospect for him.'

Dawson nodded. 'He's been the law for so long, it's the only way they *can* see him. Well, he might've been tough on folk but he's kept the town safe for families. That ought to earn him respect and if he's got that, reckon it counts for a helluva lot.'

She looked at him steadily, suddenly realizing that Matt Dawson, and all the other drifters who kept the cattle industry flourishing, were probably heading for the same kind of future – born loners, independent, stubborn in their ways, painfully self-sufficient. Not much to look forward to.

Then the marshal rode in and dismounted stiffly, each move punctuated with a grunt. He leaned against his sweating horse and mopped his face with a neckerchief. He squinted at the climbing sun.

'Kinda early for me to be up and about this far from home.'

'How does coffee and bacon and eggs sound?'

He worked up a half-grin for Eadie and pushed off the horse, tucking away the neckerchief. 'Reckon I can just about make it as far as that dogrun where I see Dawson an' Curly eatin'. How you afford to feed that boy?'

'I sometimes wonder. He's doubled his appetite since we moved the herd back into a fenced pasture. Seems to thrive on work before eating.'

'Takes more'n that to give me an appetite these days,' Britt said slowly, rubbing an aching elbow.

After he had eaten and got a pipe going, Britt thanked Eadie for a fine breakfast, then asked for details about the raid.

The three dead men were in the barn now and Britt stared at them a long time. He pointed to the man who had been backshot.

'Think I've got a dodger on him. Fancy name: Bonham? No! They call him "Bonnie" Doone, said to hail from England originally.'

'More likely Scotland with a name like that,' Eadie said.

'Could be. I seem to recall it said on the dodger he had a strange accent. Well, mebbe the devil won't be able to understand him and he'll turn him away – 'long as he don't send him back here.'

'The other two?' Dawson asked but the lawman shook his head slowly.

'Hard to tell with that feller who got trampled in the stampede and I dunno the other. Hired guns, I guess. That business about the hundred-dollar bills looks promising, though. It's not likely these three killed Luke Rafter, they'd be at the nearest big town livin' it up if they'd got his wad. All carrying the same amount is odd, though, like they been paid off. I'll check with the banker and see if those numbers match the ones you gave Rafter, Eadie.'

'There's not much hope of finding out who hired those three, I suppose?'

'Now, I wouldn't say that, Eadie. Hundred-dollar bills don't circulate in a place like Durham very much. If Luke's killer's still around, he'll want to be spending. I'll check with Bondurant at the general store. And Tate Meehan at the saloon. Could be someone's passed one of those bills.' He sighed. 'They leave many tracks?'

'None worthwhile, not after that stampede,' Dawson told him. 'Only clear ones were left by the feller Curly went after.'

'I never shot him, Marshal!' Curly said quickly, worriedly, preparing to go on herd-watch now he'd eaten.

'No, son, I know that.' Britt turned to Dawson. 'You say you saw someone riding away, on a paint horse?'

'Just a glimpse. Could've been dappled, but looked like a paint, what I could see between the rocks.'

'Then I'd better go have a word with Link Hauser. He's the only one rides a paint in these parts, and he uses a big-calibre rifle. Which don't make him any too smart if he used it to back-shoot Doone.'

'Is he the kind who'd do that?'

Britt looked levelly at Dawson. 'Link Hauser would cut his own throat if someone paid him enough.'

Matt smiled crookedly. 'That says a lot for his brains! If he's got any.'

'Like a snake.'

'You want company?'

Britt shook his head. 'Nope. But I'll smoke another pipe and see if I can talk Eadie into a little more of that bacon and a hot biscuit before I go.'

Eadie smiled. 'We don't usually serve seconds, Marshal, but I'll make a special effort for you.'

Britt smiled, the first time Dawson had seen him do so; a few years dropped away and he caught a glimpse of Britt as he must've been before the hard living had caught up with him. He might even have been reasonably good looking, but the hard, cold eyes didn't change. Or that tight *I am the law!* look.

'That damn ride all the way out from town is gonna be worth it after all,' he said, patting his stomach.

'You're a goddamn *fool*!'

Lafe Randall's harsh words brought a flush to Link Hauser's face and his thin lips clamped into a razor line.

'I done what you wanted,' he growled, looking bleakly across the dim office at Randall. 'Luke Rafter refused to sell you his place because you'd been rawhidin' him for too long. He sold to the Kern woman for just over half of what you offered, just to thumb his nose at you.'

'All right! All *right*!' Randall was not amused.

But Hauser wasn't finished: no one prodded him and called him a fool, boss or not.

'You couldn't let him get away with that, could you? So you told me to nail the stupid son of a bitch once he'd cleared the Bend. Which I did. *And* I kept the money he was carryin'. You said that was OK at the time, but you never paid me the five hundred you'd promised me for doin' the job!'

'When you'd already picked three thousand off Rafter?' Randall snorted. 'What kinda fool you take me for!'

'You really want me to tell you?'

Randall's handsome face took on the look of a thundercloud, gathering fury, a warning to all smart enough to heed. He stood up behind his desk and, although he didn't show it, Hauser felt a shaft of ice run through his tense body.

'Too damn big for your boots, Link! That's what you are. Too – damn – big, and I got no use for anyone thinks he can push his sass at me and not pay for it.'

'I'm waitin' to *get* paid! Five hundred bucks! And what you conned me into payin' them hardcases outta Rafter's wad—'

'I told you I'm strapped for ready cash. You're better off anyway – three thousand against five hundred, for Chris'sakes! What's your beef?'

'Ah, I've had enough! To hell with you all. I'm quittin' Rockin' R'. As of now!'

Randall stiffened, more alarmed than he allowed to show at his ramrod's words. Hell, Link Hauser knew too much about his business to let him go all riled like this.

'Take it easy, Link!' Randall stood and came round the desk. Hauser was on his feet quickly, his right hand easing towards his gun butt. The rancher drew himself up, mighty wary. 'Hey, come on! We've had our differences before.'

No reaction from Hauser – except to let his right hand actually rest on the butt of his Colt. Randall's tongue flickered across his lips.

'Look, things would've been all right if you hadn't used one of the hundred-dollar bills in town. After payin' them three fools outta the same batch. Not too bright, Link.'

'I wanted a telescope sight for my Sharps; been after one for years, and Mitcham had just got one in. Eighty-nine dollars and some cents. I never had that much in ready cash, but I had the money from Rafter.

I didn't aim to miss out, 'cause he told me it was the only one he had and couldn't get any more—'

'Just making sure he got the sale! He's got another one in his gunshop window now! I saw it yesterday.'

Luke scowled. 'Yeah! The wrangler told me about it. Maybe I'll pay that slimy gunmaker a visit before I leave.'

'And mebbe you won't! Britt'll get on to it, the way he does, and then we'll have real trouble – or you will.'

Link Hauser smiled crookedly. 'If I got trouble, so've you, Lafe, you know that damn well.'

Randall kept his face as composed as he could, which wasn't as good as he thought. He sighed. 'Look, I can likely rake up five hundred from the ranch safe. But that's all I've got on hand. Then he added, bitterly, 'It ought to be enough to get you on your way with whatever's left from Rafter.'

Hauser stared back coldly. 'I'm short what them three hardcases were paid, thanks to you connin' me. And now it's got us into a whole slew of trouble!'

Randall tensed, he hadn't thought about the hundred-dollar bills being traced when he'd talked Link round to forking out nine hundred bucks. But he hadn't expected the raid on Eadie's to go so wrong, either. And he knew damn well how dangerous and unpredictable Hauser could be.

'I'll take whatever you've got in the safe and vamoose, Lafe,' Hauser said, as if confirming what was passing through Randall's mind. 'You better hope Britt don't catch up with me.'

Randall stiffened. 'If he catches up with you, he

won't give you time to talk your way out of it.'

Hauser snorted. 'He's goin' soft in his old age! Hell, I seen him ridin' through Twobit Pass not long ago and I coulda blowed him outta the saddle. He was half-asleep! Wouldn't know if he rode over a cliff till he tried to fly.'

'I wouldn't write him off just yet, Link. But if somethin' did happen to him this basin'd be a whole lot easier to fix the way I want it.'

Link smiled crookedly. 'You makin' me an offer?'

Randall scrubbed a hand across his square jaw.

'You go get your gear. Lemme think about it a little. We might be able to do each other a good turn, Link.'

' 'Long as it pays good, I'm interested.'

It was mid-afternoon when Marshal Britt rode into Rocking R. Randall had seen him coming and was on the porch to greet him. He was holding a bottle of whiskey and two shot glasses.

'Hell, you better step down and have a shot of whiskey, Lyndon! You look plumb tuckered.'

The lawman's face was pale with a tinge of grey. He dismounted slowly and leaned heavily on his mount. 'Rid more miles today than I have for months. I'll take you up on the whiskey, just as soon as I crawl into that chair right beside you.'

Britt sighed as he sank into the cane chair, put his head back and closed his eyes, but opened them when he heard the rancher filling the glasses. The rancher gave him a glass full to the brim and he sipped gratefully.

'Hits the spot. Link around?'

Randall straightened out his face. 'No, Lyndon, he's gone. Quit on me.'

Britt came alert. 'Sudden, wasn't it?'

'Yeah. We had a few words. Fact we've been edgy with each other for some time. He's so damn hungry for money! Yet he seems to have plenty – bought some fancy telescope sight for his rifle.'

'I know – paid for it with a hundred-dollar bill.'

Randall whistled softly. 'Where the hell did *he* get a hundred-dollar bill?'

'What I wanted to ask him. Tell you why I'm interested.'

Watching the rancher closely without seeming to, Britt told the story of the three raiders at Box K, and how all were carrying hundred-dollar bills. 'Traced them to the ones Luke Rafter was carryin' when he was dry-gulched. It's my opinion Link knows somethin' about Luke's killing. And how come these raiders were carrying hundred-dollar bills in the same series of numbers as he paid the gunsmith?'

'Judas priest! Hell, he's been pretty damn rough with the men lately, then ridin' off for a couple days at a time, no explanation. *Then* he asks for a goddam raise!' Randall shook his head, tight-lipped. 'I told him, he's not happy with what I pay him now, he better quit.' He smiled ruefully. 'He called my bluff! Didn't want to lose him, 'cause he's a good cowman once he shakes them bad moods.' He shrugged. 'But he up and left.'

Britt finished his glass and held it out for a refill. He

signed for Randall to stop when the glass was half-full. 'Where was he headed?'

'Not sure. He went up towards the Organ Pipes, so he could be thinkin' of cutting through Hashknife and mebbe goin' on to Catamount.'

Britt frowned. 'He know anyone up there?'

'We-ell, Link knows folk all over. An' some none too savoury.'

'Like the Petty brothers at the old Catamount swing station.'

'Well, I dunno, Lyndon. I mean, I know the Pettys step over the mark every so often but whether Link knows 'em, I'm not sure.'

'Well, Lafe, I need to talk with Link. Can you get someone to rub down my horse and give him a little grain, and a small extra bag for me to carry, too? Then I'll get goin'.'

'Sure, I can fix that.' Randall kept the worried look on his face. 'But I can put you up overnight, Lyndon. You can do with a rest.'

'Won't give you an argument there, but longer I stay round here, further Link gets ahead of me. But, of course, you realize that already, don't you?'

Randall's face straightened. 'I'll get someone to rub down your hoss,' he said stiffly. He stepped down from the porch and strode across the yard.

Because the sun was so low as he entered the jumble of mostly vertical rock columns known as the Organ Pipes, Lyndon Britt saw the flash, and figured right away it was from the lens of a set of field glasses – or maybe of a telescope sight.

He slammed his mount sideways as a big-calibre rifle boomed, its thunder seeming to shake the rocks and make the air tremble. Britt moved stiffly and wasn't quick enough quitting the saddle before the rifle boomed again. He felt the hammer-blow on his upper left arm. It spun him as he was halfway free of the stirrup, twisted his slim body and dumped him unceremoniously in a rough rectangle of low rocks.

It was small and he was lucky he didn't strike the rocks, but landed on the patch of dirt. It shook him up, lights dancing behind his eyes, his rheumaticky joints creaking and jarring painfully. Not to mention his wounded arm.

He was surprised that he had instinctively grabbed his rifle as he quit leather and, a shade breathless now, eased in close against the front row of rocks.

The next bullet spattered only six inches in front of his face and bits of hot lead stung him. But he brought his Winchester up and raked the only clear piece of rim he could see with a volley of five fast shots.

He heard some of his bullets ricocheting, and next time Link Hauser's big Sharps spoke it was from the left and higher up, from where he could see down into the marshal's ring of rocks. When the next bullet gouged into the gravel beside him, Britt knew Hauser had the better of him. The much sought-after high ground.

He rolled away into shadow, hoping he could hold out till it grew dark, which shouldn't be long now. He was a damn fool for riding into this winding maze they called Hashknife so late in the day. Once it was dark, he wouldn't be able to find his way out. But Hauser was high enough up to see at least some of the trails and keep him pinned down.

Britt knew he had literally ridden into a dead end – with the emphasis on the 'dead'.

He had to get out of this rock square, anyway. His heart was hammering, but occasionally it would falter and he felt momentarily dizzy. But self-preservation drove him on and when there was a break in the shooting – Hauser no doubt reloading – Lyndon Britt heaved up and threw himself over the rocks

Something like an iron fist clenched his heart, and he couldn't breathe. There was a searing light behind his eyes, his chest felt as if his horse was standing on it and his arms were tingling, then numb and useless. He fell on his face, saliva trickling from the corner of his slack mouth.

But things couldn't be too bad, he thought vaguely, because someone laughed.

Then Hauser's big rifle thundered twice. But Britt only heard the first shot.

His heart had stopped even before the bullet slammed into his old body, so hard that the impact threw him halfway across the rocks, where he lay as if his back was broken.

Link Hauser stood up now and put two more shots into the jerking body.

'Be of good heart, Marshal!' he said aloud, chuckling even as he searched for the lawman's horse. He levered another cartridge into the drop-down breech.

But the horse was too smart; it made its way into the maze, giving itself at least some cover. It angered Link that some dumb animal could even try to outsmart him. Then he grinned; he could just make out the horse in the fading light. He sighted carefully and fired.

'Not so smart after all, you damn jughead!'

CHAPTER 8

SET-UP

Matt Dawson might have been the lightest sleeper in the Box K bunkhouse but Spanish wasn't far behind. As Dawson padded to the door and eased it ajar, cocked six-gun in. his hand, he heard Spanish getting out of his bunk, asking in a hushed voice,

'Trouble?'

'Not sure.' Dawson raised his voice. 'Call out! Two seconds and I start shooting!'

'Hey, hold up!' a nervous voice called out of the darkness. 'I'm Ben Skene, wrangler at Rocking R.'

'What're you doing here?'

'Got somethin' you might like to see.'

'I'll bet. Light a match and show me.'

Skene laughed shortly. 'Sure! An' make a great target! Listen, I was doin' nighthawk and choused what I thought was a damn scrub bull sniffin' round Mr Randall's heifers in the creek pasture – but I was wrong. This hoss come trottin' up, whinnyin' kind of sad, you know? Like it was hurt an' wanted company.'

'You're too damn long winded, Skene! Get on with it!'

'OK! It *is* hurt. Looks like a bullet burn across the hip, blood all over the place. I was just across the crick from your pasture with the busted fence and it kind of headed over that way, so I followed it and edged it in up here.'

'Now why would you do that?'

'Well – it – it looks like Marshal Britt's mount to me.'

Dawson opened the door all the way. 'Cover me, Spanish.'

Curly was awake now but Alec Crewe was nighthawking. The man from Rocking R sounded nervous and Dawson could see he sat his saddle with hands raised now.

'Listen. I ain't up to anythin'! I don't like to see hosses sufferin' an' – this place was close. Miss Eadie's always been good with animals and I thought. . . .'

Dawson and Spanish ignored him, the latter striking a match while Curly nervously held a rifle on Ben Skene.

'See? It's got that blaze face like the Marshal's mount. An' he's sure travelled some by the looks of him.'

'Bullet gouge, all right. Be painful but it won't cripple him,' Dawson said, shaking out the first vesta and lighting another. 'I think it's the same mount Britt was forking when he left here yest'y afternoon.'

'Yeah, it's Britt's sorrel,' Spanish said definitely. 'Put your hands down, Ben, for God's sake. We ain't gonna shoot you.'

'That new feller sounded like he wanted to,' Skene said, looking at Dawson as he lowered his arms.

'Not right now,' Dawson assured him. 'You see which way the hoss came from?'

Skene thought about it. 'Workin' it out from where I was when I first heard the heifers gettin' nervous, I'd say – well, from the direction of the Organ Pipes, I guess.'

'What would Britt be doing up there, Spanish?'

'Dunno. Might've been goin' after someone.' Spanish looked sharply at Skene. 'Yeah! That's right. Britt was goin' to Rocking R to talk with Link Hauser. He workin' up near the Pipes, Ben?'

'He's not workin' anywheres for Randall. He quit this afternoon – and. . . .' Skene stopped, and there was enough light for Dawson to see his tongue flicker over his lips.

'What?'

'He – he's got friends up in Catamount.'

Dawson, frowning, glanced at Spanish.

'Old swing station; bunch of hardcases hang out there – the Petty brothers. Make nuisances of themselves hittin' the spreads or an occasional stage coach. You ride through the Organ Pipes and Hashknife Pass to get there.'

Eadie came out now, a gown tied about her waist covering her night attire. She held a large pistol in her hands which Dawson identified as a Big Dragoon

91

cap-and-ball Colt. They kicked like a mule, but could knock that same mule clear off its feet if you shot straight enough.

Spanish explained what Skene was doing here and Eadie examined the wounded horse.

'Get him into the barn, Spanish, and I'll do what I can for him.'

I – I'd like to stay an' help, Miz Kern, but – well, I guess Randall wouldn't take kindly to me leavin' my nighthawk post to bring Marshal Britt's hoss to you.'

'It was good of you to take the trouble, Ben. Would you like some coffee before you go?'

'I sure would. But I better not. Hope that sorrel's OK, ma'am. I – think he should be. But I dunno as I'd like to say the same about Marshal Britt.'

They were silent as Skene rode off.

'If Britt was trailing Hauser into those Organ Pipes and his horse is here, bullet-gouged,' Dawson said slowly, 'I wouldn't like to hazard a guess about how well he is right now, either.'

'Well, if you're thinkin' Britt's been dry-gulched, I gotta tell you, it'd be right in Link Hauser's line. He's a right dangerous son of a – sorry, Eadie,' Spanish said.

'What can we do?' the girl asked, as she and Dawson followed Spanish into the barn with the limping sorrel.

'*I* can go try to find him. I don't know the country but I can track good as most Indians.'

She looked at Matt in the doorway of the barn as Spanish lit a lantern and hung it on a nail on a post by its wire handle. 'Link Hauser's got a bad reputation, and there's no doubt the horse has been shot.'

'No doubt at all,' Matt agreed readily. 'One other thing you don't know about me, Eadie. I used to be a bounty hunter, long time ago.'

She looked at him steadily. 'You're – just full of surprises, aren't you, Matt?'

He smiled faintly. 'Just hope I can surprise Hauser.'

'I've got a very good geological survey map. It's well-creased but it'll help you find your way through that maze of canyons and draws and dead-ends. It could be very dangerous, though, Matt.'

'You get the map while I change, and make sure my guns are loaded.'

'Yes! *Please* do that!'

The map Eadie had given him was the latest US Geological Survey map, a year old, and it covered the entire Basin.

So, even if Hauser managed to wipe out his trail, at least Dawson would be able to find his way around in that rugged country. There was always the possibility of ambush, but the map was detailed enough for him to see at a glance some places where dry-gulching could be set up effectively.

He left Box K while it was still dark and, following Spanish's directions, he found his way to a ledge this side of Hashknife Pass where he could hole up until daylight under an overhang. From there he could get a good view of the pass before venturing into it.

'Don't underestimate Hauser,' Spanish warned.

'There's talk of him havin' been mixed up in several killin's. Britt's had his eye on him for a long time.'

With this information under his belt, Matt Dawson rode out on his dappled dun, yawning, but knowing he had better make sure he was wide awake for this chore.

Or he could be sleeping the Big Sleep from which there was no awakening. . . .

He slept fitfully but was alert and eating a cold breakfast before the sun was fully over the Organ Pipes.

Munching the last of a biscuit, he sat there and watched the light strengthen, the shadows taking on solid shapes and density, the outlines of rocks and entrances to draws and gulches becoming more clearly etched.

He wasn't high enough to have an overall view, but he checked what he could see against the map and found the location without trouble. An area labelled 'Breakbone Hill'.

'Sounds like a good place to stay away from.'

He hunkered down behind a rock now, for it was light enough for anyone in that country to see him on this ledge. There was a way down that would keep the bulk of a jutting spur of rock between him and any observer among those hills and he took it without delay, riding with his rifle across his thighs. He had to dismount in some parts and lead the reluctant dun around trail ledges that seemed not much wider than his hatbrim. But they made it down to broken ground at the base of a butte that he figured had to be at the western end of Hashknife Pass.

The rock walls reared against the sky, seemed ready to topple as clouds began to move under the thrust of air currents, high up, enhancing the illusion. Below was a rough, stone-studded trail around the base and he carefully worked the mount towards this and started into the eerie pass. He could see a strip of sky high above but deep shadow filled the pass itself. Which was maybe why he didn't see the dry-gulcher.

The bullet flicked dust from his hatbrim and in an instant he followed the hat to the ground, banging against the narrow wall. The rifle was almost jarred from his grip but he retained it, scooped his hat up and slapped it across the dun's underbelly as it started to stomp. With a snort it gathered itself and ran on, disappearing around a bend into the pass proper.

Dawson rolled in tight against the wall, a slight bulge of rock giving him some protection from above. The rifle up there hammered in a savage, wild volley, and he knew right off, it wasn't Hauser. The Sharps would have made a heavier, booming sound, couldn't shoot as fast as the Winchester, and, if Hauser still had his telescopic sight, his shots would have found a mark.

As it was, sand and grit stung Matt's face and he clamped his eyes closed swiftly, tried to edge back even more, but the rock stopped him. Half-deafened by the gunfire, he brought his own rifle round, then realized that the man above must be reloading in this sudden hiatus.

A moment's pause, and then he took a chance that

could have cost him his life.

He wriggled out and ran to the far side of the pass; it was only a few yards here but a good marksman might have picked him off. He slammed hard into the rock, the breath knocked out of him in a harsh burst. Up there, thirty feet above, he could see the rifle barrel moving about as the killer frantically thumbed home cartridges into the tube magazine.

Breathing hard but steadily, Dawson pressed back into a small dark cavity, rifle cocked, waiting.

It was only seconds before the head and one shoulder showed up there as the man sighted his rifle. Matt smiled a little as the man stiffened when he couldn't find his target where he expected it. His head snapped around to his own side and he eased forward to look over and down.

Matt shot him in the head. He had to duck back as the rifle fell with a clatter, knocking handfuls of gravel and dust from the wall above. The man himself did not fall, but one arm was dangling over the edge. Dawson's mouth tightened as he recognized the green-checked sleeve of the shirt; it was the one Ben Skene had worn back at Box K.

'So, it was all a set-up to get me in here.'

Skene was likely meant to drive Dawson into the waiting guns of Link Hauser, but the wrangler had tried to kill Matt himself, inadvertently giving him warning.

Lyndon Britt's mount *had* been bullet-burned, so the marshal could still be lying badly hurt out here somewhere or, more probably, dead.

And Dawson had to find out, even if he risked riding into another dry-gulching.

After studying the map again he suddenly leapt into the saddle of the startled dun and rammed home his blunted, rowelless spurs. He lay low over the dun's straining neck, the mane whipping into his face, his hat hanging down his back by the rawhide tie-thong.

He used the rein ends to lash at the startled horse – it wasn't used to such rough treatment – but he felt the moving muscles bunch and gather and the speed increased. Then he wrenched the reins to the left. The horse had no sooner veered that way than he hauled the reins hard right.

The dun snorted and belly-growled to let him know this kind of treatment was not acceptable, but still it obeyed.

In minutes he was through the pass, having zigzagged wildly. The fact that there hadn't been any shooting from above meant one of two things: his move had caught Hauser off-guard if he was up on the rim, or he wasn't there at all and the manoeuvre had not been necessary. No! With a man like Hauser after your hide, any method of throwing him off was necessary.

Once through he saw that the ground sloped away now from this end of the pass and then swooped up again towards a cluster of tall, partly rounded rock columns of varying heights. These had to be the Organ Pipes and he felt that old itch between his shoulder blades that warned him: here lay the real threat, danger of the deadliest kind.

The sun was high now, hot across his back and hands and the metal of the Winchester rapidly grew warm. He still had a little height here and used it to his advantage by stopping the dun behind a rock, then climbing up to stand on the saddle, hat off, easing his head up so it wouldn't be silhouetted against the pulsing blue sky. He moved his gaze slowly, sorting out blurred colours, quirky shadows that made ordinary rocks look like a gloved hand, or part of a turning head, even the edge of a shoulder.

No. Hauser was well hidden if he was down there.

Then something caught his eye where the trail took a swing around a corner of granite boulders. Something was on the ground, not fully visible, but it looked like the lower legs of a man. He could make out dirty brown corduroy trousers – and boots: boots of a distinctive kind. Britt wore ankle boots with special inserts of strong elastic on the sides because of his rheumatics. They were easier to put on and take off, more comfortable for walking around town, which he did a lot more than he rode these days. The hell with why Britt wore them: he did – so it meant that was him lying out there, and he had to be unconscious – or dead.

Dawson gripped the gun more tightly, looking around the lower levels for an ambush spot, tensed and ready to shoot. No-ooo – it seemed clear, but. . . .

He should have looked above, almost straight up.

The booming thunder of the Sharps overflowed the canyon and beat at his ears an instant before the bullet seared his back, high up, and knocked him sprawling from the dun's saddle.

The horse stomped and shied and maybe it saved his life, its big body shielding him from the second shot. But the bullet clipped the dun's right ear, blood sprayed, and it took off whickering, leaving Dawson exposed on the shale.

He lay there, his rifle a good two feet from his hand, blood staining his shirt, a drumming tattoo of pain coursing through his shoulders and neck and down his left arm,

Somehow he managed to tilt over on to his left side, – and it hurt like the devil! Through dimming vision he saw the man who was going to kill him. He was up on the rim, on one knee, the big rifle resting on a rock as he edged around to get into the right position for drawing a bead on the wounded man sprawled awkwardly beside the rocks.

Matt Dawson knew he was a breath from dying, and here a ricochet would be more deadly than a direct hit.

With a wrenching effort that sent hot pain searing through his entire body, he drew his Colt, clamped his benumbed left hand over the right which was already gripping the butt. Gritting his teeth, he fired three ragged shots at the killer on the rim. Rock chips flew from the edge, dust spurting into Hauser's face. He fired and his upper body jerked with the recoil of the big Sharps, but his aim was off now, and he had to take time to wipe dust and grit angrily from his eyes.

Dawson couldn't stay where he was. So far he had been lucky and he would like nothing better than to ease back and close his eyes, to try to forget the pain that enveloped his entire upper body. But if he did he was a dead man.

So he crawled back deeper into the rocks, found a small cleft and, groaning, lowered himself into it as far as he could go. His upper body was exposed but he found that an advantage: he could rest his elbow on the rock and steady his six-gun.

He had to remember – only three shots left.

He saw Hauser up there now and could imagine the man's curses as he moved this way and that, trying to get the best position for a killing shot.

Then Matt blinked, not only to clear his clouding vision, but in total surprise.

Hauser was climbing down! Then he saw the small jutting flat rock about ten feet below the rim. It was wide enough to allow Hauser to move right or left, and so possibly get an opening where he could shoot directly into the fissure where Dawson crouched.

The man even paused to look down, and called, 'I'm comin' for you, gunfighter!'

'Yeah. Come – on – down!' Matt gasped but figured it wasn't loud enough for the words to reach the killer.

No matter!

He steadied his Colt in both hands and fired, twice, the gun almost jumping from his weakening grip.

Link Hauser came down to him with a rush that ended in a sodden thump that rapped the man's head hard half a dozen times before one arm flung across part of Dawson's fissure, the lacerated fingers jerking briefly.

Matt's last thought before the blackness enfolded him was that there was a hell of a lot of blood.

And some of it was his.

Maybe too much.

CHAPTER 9

THE DEAD AND
THE DYING

There were voices. Different voices. One at least was a woman's, but there was too much background noise for him to hear what they were saying.

Slowly, the darkness eased behind his eyes and there was a red tone which somehow he knew was caused by light shining through his closed eyelids.

So he opened them, tentatively, the lashes streaking the scene awaiting him for a moment before they cleared the pupils' area and he was able look up at a ceiling, rough tarpaper painted over a long time ago, some patches bare – but he recognized it.

It was the ceiling of Doc Fallon's infirmary, He was not a prosperous medical practitioner, simply because his style was not to charge the poor and he barely cleared expenses with other patients. He had a small private income but it did not allow for ostentatious presentation; he figured putting the money into medicines and better equipment was more important. His grateful patients thought so, too.

'So you've decided to join us.'

Fallon's voice reached down through the thick cobwebs dulling Dawson's mind and he blinked. The action cleared his vision and he saw a strange woman standing beside the doctor. She wore a white smock and her sleeves were rolled up, small hands were now holding some bloodstained bandages. He must have been staring because she smiled, the action lighting up a square-jawed face with warm brown eyes under a cap of light brown hair.

'I'm Julia, the doctor's daughter. I also double as nurse on occasion. How're you feeling?'

'Like I been shot high up in the back.'

She laughed briefly. 'Then you are fully conscious, wouldn't you agree, Father?'

'Yes, he's rejoined us.' Doc Fallon leaned over the bed. 'Large-calibre bullet. Clipped your shoulder and gouged part of your back. Obviously hit you from above. If it had hit squarely, it would've taken your left arm off.'

He was serious now and the nurse's smile slowly faded. Matt nodded. 'Link Hauser's Sharps.'

'Yes. Spanish and Curly brought him in, along with Ben Skene and Marshal Britt. All three are dead, but I only feel for Lyndon Britt. You're the only survivor.'

'I saw Britt's legs sticking out of some rocks. Guess Hauser left him there to get my attention while he drew a bead on me.'

'That sounds like the way Hauser would think. You're a very tough and efficient man, Matt.'

'Had some luck, Doc, and a good map that Eadie gave me.'

'Yes, your things are there in that cupboard beside your bed,' Julia Fallon told him. 'But you call me by ringing that small bell on the shelf and I'll get what you want. You mustn't go twisting your body just yet.'

He hated the thought of depending on other people for help with such trivial things, but the way his left shoulder and side felt, he'd have to do it, for a short time.

'Eadie knows all about it, I guess?' When the doc nodded, he asked, 'How long was I out, anyway?'

'Just over twenty-four hours. You lost a good deal of blood. There was a little fever, too, but you've shaken it. You've made a strong recovery so far.'

'My horse?'

'In the livery. Just a nicked ear which Eadie tended, she being the closest thing we have to a veterinarian in this neck of the woods.'

They saw he was relieved to know his dun was all right and Fallon gave him one more mental tick; a man who thinks of his horse when he's been wounded like Dawson and had to be suffering real pain – well, he was one to ride the river with in the sawbones's book.

'How long will I be here?'

Julia and her father exchanged a glance and Fallon smiled thinly. 'I told Julia it would be one of the first questions you asked. That shoulder's going to be stiff for some time and there'll be a deal of swelling and a lot of pain before it's back to normal. I'll give you some exercises.'

'Long as it gets back to normal, Doc.' He raised his head a little and winced as the movement made his neck muscles shoot barbs of hot pain. He was trying to see who else was in the infirmary, which was set up to take four beds, though after a bad twister once it had taken ten, and the number of patients had been doubled by laying straw mattresses for them beneath the real beds.

Right now he seemed to be the only patient. 'Business not so good?'

'Believe it or not, it's how we prefer it,' Julia told him, smiling again as she rearranged his pillows. She looked sharply at him as he gasped involuntarily with pain. 'I'm sorry, but even the slightest movement will hurt for another day or so.'

He asked for the map. She got it from the bedside cupboard and he started to thank her, but the words slurred and he drifted down into a recuperative sleep.

Next time he opened his eyes, lamps were burning and the room was full of shadows. Eadie sat in a cane chair near the foot of his bed, leafing through a tattered *Harper's Weekly*. When she heard him stir she smiled and came down beside him, arranging the sheet which he had pushed down during his sleep.

'Glad to see you're conscious! You were breathing so shallowly I . . . sort of panicked and shouted for the doctor. Julia came in and reassured me you were still alive – I'm sorry you had so much trouble, Matt.'

'I went looking for it. Just glad I walked away – well, got carried away, afterwards.'

She had brought him some biscuits and a slice of cake she had baked, and he munched, at first to please her, but then he realized he was ravenous. Eadie read the signs and went to arrange a meal for him, which Julia brought in shortly afterwards.

'A little light-on for a start, Mr Dawson. Some cold cuts and mashed potatoes and peas, but the coffee's strong.'

'Help me sit up! I need that java.'

While he ate, Doc Fallon came hurrying in, and then Julia with armfuls of bed linen. Eadie had gone out, too, but came back now, with her arms loaded with pillows. The two women started to makeup the vacant beds.

'What's wrong?' Matt asked around the last mouthful of cold beef.

'Been a bad accident out at Rocking R,' Fallon told him. 'You're going to have company, though I doubt from what I've been told they'll be talking to you; not for a while at least, if ever.'

'What kind of accident, Doc?'

Fallon paused in setting out instruments, turned to look at Dawson, frowning. 'I believe it was some kind of . . . explosion. Blasting rock and tree stumps to clear a new pasture. But one charge went off prematurely and three of Randall's men were badly injured. They're on their way in now. One of his men rode on ahead to alert us.'

The rest was chaos – or so it seemed to Dawson.

He lay there, virtually ignored as everyone seemed to rush about without design; but that was OK by him: he felt better for his long sleep and the food and toyed with the map, studying it, though not fully taking in what he was seeing. His body was still recovering from the shock of the wound and the pain was taking a lot more of his attention than he realized, intruding on his concentration.

Around him, Doc Fallon, in a bloodstained apron and with Julia and Eadie helping, was treating the injured men. None of them was conscious. Their injuries were substantial; two had crushed chests. He heard Fallon say they would be lucky to pull through. The other had badly broken legs, as well as other serious contusions and fractures.

'Will he be able to walk again, Father?' Julia asked.

Fallon shook his head irritably as he pulled out some bloody slivers of bone with dripping tweezers. 'Not without crutches, maybe not at all. That head wound is quite serious, too.'

'It must've been a bad explosion,' Julia commented. Eadie, passing at that moment with her arms full of the bloody, dirt-clogged clothes removed from the victims, paused, frowning.

'Yes. I was wondering why we hadn't heard any blasting on Box K. They could've been working over the far side of Rocking R, of course, but usually dynamite can be heard even at that distance. It resembles rumbling thunder, but I've heard nothing.'

'Well, it seems to have brought down a lot of rubble,' said Doc Fallon. 'The amount of dirt and filth on these men, especially in their hair, is consistent with a whole blamed mountain falling on them. But how is not important right now. I ... I'm afraid I might have to amputate this one's lower leg. The bone is pulverized.'

The smell of chloroform from Fallon's operating room right next door to the bed section made Dawson queasy; it was the one thing he had hated about being a field medic. He tried hard to concentrate on the survey map, not knowing what he was looking at, or why. The mingled odours of blood and body fluids, plus the anaesthetic and antiseptics got to him, brought back disturbing memories of those bloody war years. He asked if he could be moved on to the side veranda.

Fallon was annoyed at the interruption but Eadie volunteered to move him while Julia assisted with the operations on all three victims. There was an iron-wheeled chair with a wicker seat and arms and Julia came and lent a hand to get Dawson into it. Even before Eadie had pushed him out into the fresh air, he was half-asleep, the pain roaring through his upper body.

The night passed in a series of disturbances; the women and Fallon rushed about, clattering instruments in metal bowls, dropping this, that or the other item; once he heard the sound of breaking glass. A man screamed in the early hours and it faded eventually to end in sobbing; later he learned it was the cowhand who had lost his lower leg.

Dawson drifted in and out of shallow sleep and it grew cold on the veranda, but he awoke one time to find that someone had draped a heavy blanket over him. The warmth allowed him to have a better sleep and it was sunlight that eventually woke him: early sunlight.

The smells of the night were still heavy on the air but somehow his stomach had begun to accept them. When Eadie brought him strong coffee and bacon and eggs he started to feel more alive.

She looked grey and drawn, dark shadows under her eyes.

'You ought to put your head down somewhere and get some sleep, Eadie. You look worn out.'

'Julia is standing up to it better than me and Doc Fallon must be close to exhaustion but he refuses to stop. They still need me to help for a while yet.'

'How're the men?'

She shook her head. 'Two are critical, Doc says. The third will probably pull through, eventually. They want to set up a bed for you out here as there'll be a lot of activity inside there.'

'Whatever Doc wants. I'm not too bad. You staying on?'

'No, I'll head back to Box K. I'll try to get in sometime later in case I'm wanted.'

As she made to leave, he reached out and took her lower arm. She looked at him puzzled. 'Can you bring – or send in that old Spanish map?'

Her frown deepened.'Ye-es. Any special reason?'

'Aw, just thought I'd amuse myself trying to match some of the survey map details with the original. Can't do much else, and it'll help fill in the time.'

'I'll either send it in with Spanish or Alec or bring it myself when I come. Now you get some rest, too. I know you aren't as well as you try to make out.'

'Next time you visit, I'll be dangerous, so watch out.'

She smiled, but seemed a little surprised at his attempt at levity. Here was one very tough man!

During the next three days, two of the Rocking R men died. The one with the badly crushed chest was the first, but the other man with a similar injury was still hanging on. The second man to die was the cowboy who had had his lower leg amputated.

'It was a very bad injury but I'd had every hope of his recovery,' Doc Fallon said, his genuine grief obvious. He shook his head wonderingly. 'I believe he simply couldn't face the prospect of being one-legged; just – gave up.'

Dawson let the doctor talk on about the injuries; his own wound was healing well but still stiff and painful, even more so after the mild exercises Fallon insisted on Matt doing in order to stall off any permanent restrictions to shoulder movement.

'Doc, those injuries on the others. . . ?' Fallon snapped his head up at Dawson's querying tone. Their eyes met, and held; Dawson felt that the man already knew what he was about to say. 'Any of those fellers have their backs hurt?'

'All three, since you ask.' Fallon spoke quietly, still watching Dawson's serious face. 'Not only that, all three had wounds to the backs of their heads. One was very bad, on the man who had the worst-crushed chest.'

'Almost like they'd been – stooping, bending over, when they were hurt? Something – heavy – fell on 'em. . . ?'

'Exactly like that. You're remembering your field medic training, I see.'

'Something you never forget, Doc. But it was you saying they had their hair choked with dirt, and down inside their clothes. I saw a lot of casualties from varying types of explosions in the War; they all had small stones or grit driven into their skin, just under the surface. You never mentioned that on those Rocking R men.'

'Because, as you have no doubt deduced, there wasn't any sign of gravel or grit driven under the skin. Almost as if the explosion – if that's what it was – happened above them, injuring backs, lower bodies, the rear of the skulls. Is that what you wanted to hear?'

'Dunno that I wanted to hear it, particularly, but those men showed all the signs of having been caught in a cave-in, Doc, like a tunnel collapse, or a mine shaft.'

Fallon jerked his head up. 'Mine shaft! It must be a hundred years since they gave up looking for any gold or silver or payable minerals of any kind in this basin.' His words slowly trailed off. 'Unless – unless someone discovered an old abandoned mine.'

111

'On Rocking R?'

'That's anybody's guess, but I've never heard of it. And Lafe Randall's not the kind of man who'd waste time and money, working an ancient mine that had never produced in the first place.'

'Well, that's the general belief, Doc. But the Old Spaniards, the original settlers of the Grant, might've encouraged that belief; that there was no worthwhile gold to be had. Mexico City is a helluva long way off, but they collected their taxes from all over, never missed a *peso* or even a *centavo*. If some Spaniard way up here, hundreds of miles from Mexico City, could line his coffers with gold he hadn't declared or paid taxes on he'd be mighty rich, and could be on his way back to Spain before the tax collectors woke up.'

Fallon was silent for a short time, then shook his head slowly. 'It's all conjecture, Matt, nothing more.'

'Those injuries were real enough – ask the man still living, 'Fact, he might even say how he got 'em.'

'No! No, Matt, the man's critical. There will be no interrogation!'

'Reckoned that'd be your attitude, Doc, and that's fine with me.' Dawson reached down under the bed-clothes and brought out two thick, folded papers. He held up one, the thinner of the two. 'Geological Survey map.' Then, indicating the other: 'Old map of the original Spanish Grant.' He unfolded both, spreading them out on the makeshift bed on the veranda. 'Lots of fancy illustrations on the Spanish map, as they preferred in the eighteenth century. See here? And here. . . ?' He pointed to two faded and blurred drawings. 'Reckon they could indicate old mine entrances?'

Fallon pursed his lips. 'With some imagination, I suppose so. They could just as easily indicate camp-sites where there was water and graze.'

Dawson smiled. 'Now don't insult me like that, Doc! There's the timbers shoring the roof, see? Kinda square, dark oblongs in the centre, like entrances—'

'You've better eyes than I have!'

Dawson nodded slowly. 'OK, Doc, have it your way. But can you read that word? It's badly smeared but. . . ?'

'Looks like "door" or something – misspelled and a sort of – oh, it's a figure "5" behind it. . . . Door Five?'

'It's *D'Oro*, Doc. Gold! And the "figure" is the Spanish query mark, upside down compared to ours. See!'

Then Fallon *could* see the query mark '¿' upside down in the Spanish way. He sighed. 'Well, they would've been long abandoned, Matt. But I see what you're getting at. It's not readily obvious, but I suppose those "entrances" if that's what they are, would be somewhere on Rocking R land?'

'Yeah, I think so, Doc. Bit hard to be sure, but I've been shown around Box K, which lies pretty close to that area, and I'm sure there's no sign of old mines on it.'

Fallon, took out a pipe and packed it, obviously thinking while doing so. He lit up and puffed.

'Well, I've heard Randall is strapped for cash. But I doubt that he'd be desperate enough to think he could find gold after all this time.'

'Gold don't go away, Doc, unless someone digs it up and takes it away.'

Through the cloud of tobacco smoke Fallon said quietly, 'You've got some sort of theory, haven't you?'

'Not a theory; maybe a possibility, is all. No matter what else, Doc, you can't get away from the fact that those men were crushed in a cave-in of some sort. I worked on two tunnel collapses during the War and all the men had the same sort of injuries as Randall's crew. Now, you'll admit to that, won't you?'

Fallon puffed, looking hard at Dawson. 'Perhaps. But if you're going to use me to start more trouble between Box K and Rocking R, I'm afraid you're out of luck.'

'Relax, Doc. I was just trying out my "theory" on you, and I think you've just told me I might be on the right track.'

Fallon stared hard. 'You'd better get well quickly, I think, Matt.'

CHAPTER 10

THREATS

Lafe Randall came to see Dawson the day they buried the two men who had died from their injuries. Hauser and Skene had been laid away two days earlier without fuss.

The other accident survivor with the badly crushed chest was hanging on, but Doc Fallon was not optimistic about the man's chances of pulling through.

Dawson was sitting up in the cane wheelchair, looking out over the part of the town which could be seen from his position. He tensed when Randall strolled on to the veranda, a half-smoked cheroot jutting from one side of his mouth. With him there was another man whom Dawson didn't recognize right away, but he picked him for a professional gunfighter. He was lean, thirties, medium tall, reasonably good clothes and with a blackstring tie held with a silver clasp at his throat. The face was hawklike, the mouth thin and unsmiling, eyes Arctic-blue chips of ice that studied Dawson closely.

'You're one hard son of a bitch to get rid of, Dawson,' were Randall's opening words.

'Middle name's "Bad Penny".'

Randall smiled faintly but the gunslinger's features never changed. The rancher jerked a thumb at the man.

'New crew member of Rocking R, Tully Squires. Heard of him?'

Dawson met the lean man's stare and nodded slightly. He sensed that it pleased Squires that he knew of him.

'Saw him twice, last year and about seven, eight months back. Once in El Paso, other time in Tucson. He killed both the idiots who challenged him.'

'One shot apiece,' Squires added, very pleased at Dawson's recollections. His voice was well-modulated, which somehow surprised Dawson. 'I never waste ammunition.'

'Me neither. What you want me to do, Randall? Welcome Squires to Durham Bend?'

The rancher smiled crookedly as he shook his head. 'Just take a look. A good look. When you get outta here, you'll see him from time to time.'

'What am I s'posed to do? Run for cover, shake him by the hand – careful to make sure it ain't his gunhand, or just say "howdy" and pass on by?' There was no reaction from either visitor and Matt let his gaze rest on Tully Squires's deadpan face. 'All or any of the foregoing OK by you?'

Squires frowned. 'You looking for trouble, *amigo*, you'll find it with me.'

'Hell, I don't hunt trouble. Get enough of it just livin' day to day. But what's your new man's function, Randall? Bodyguard, fast gun, cook, outhouse swamper. . . ?'

Squire stiffened and straightened; his head just came level with Randall's wide shoulder. Those Arctic eyes were considerably warmer now, blazing with reined-in anger that was building every time Dawson opened his mouth.

'I've never shot a man in bed – or a wheelchair. Don't mean I won't.'

Dawson acknowledged that with a shrug and pursed lips. 'Best watch my mouth, then.'

Squires relaxed a little, easing his right arm away from the single Colt holstered on his left hip, butt foremost for a crossdraw. 'Link Hauser was kin of mine. First cousin, you want to know.'

'Not high on my list of interests, you wanta know.'

Squires suddenly grinned. 'I kinda like this one, Lafe. I'm workin' up a real appetite, like I was gonna set down to a big Thanksgivin' dinner, with him the turkey.' Then the voice hardened. 'When – I'm – good – and – ready.'

'All right, Dawson. You've been warned. Just wanted you to know that no one kills my men and gets away with it.'

'Mebbe you should look after 'em better, Randall. Don't let 'em set up dry-gulches, or work in tunnels that ain't shored up properly.'

Randall's face straightened and for a moment he went very still. 'What the hell're you talkin' about, tunnels? What tunnel, for Chris'sake? There're no tunnels on Rocking R!'

'Well, a mountain fell on those men you just buried, and the one still inside in the infirmary. You likely know I was a field medic in the War. I attended two cave-ins, was caught in one myself when I was working the silver mines in the Arizona Superstitions. I can recognize injuries caused when a tunnel roof collapses.'

'Too bad the one you were in didn't fall on your head,' Squires commented.

Randall chuckled, and Dawson arched his eyebrows.

'Be a quick death; that what you specialize in, Tully?'

'I shoot 'em square in the ticker, or, if I got somethin' agin a man, I might give him his in the belly, so he takes a long time to die. I've only knowed you a few minutes, Dawson, but I think you're high on that second list.'

Squires turned to the door with a swagger and Randall 'shot' Dawson with his finger and thumb, nodding as he smiled crookedly.

'Here comes your lunch. Enjoy it, drifter. Might not be too many more.'

Eadie came to see him later that afternoon. She looked good with a ribbon in her hair, frilled white blouse and short fringed jacket, denim pants tucked into the tops of her riding-boots. He noticed she was wearing a small revolver in a leather holster that appeared to have seen a fair amount of use.

'What happened to the Dragoon?'

She smiled as she sat up on the veranda rail. 'I keep that beside my bed; too heavy to carry around.' She sobered as she added: 'I believe you've met Randall's new man.'

'We exchanged pleasantries. Seems we're gonna be seeing a lot of each other after I get out of here.'

Eadie frowned. 'Matt, don't make light of it! That's Tully Squires, and he has a terrible reputation as a hired killer. Randall would never have dared bring him here when Lyndon Britt was marshal.'

'I've seen him in action.'

'You don't sound impressed.'

'Oh, he impressed me, all right – as half-brother to a bolt of lightning when it comes to a fast draw, and with about as much conscience as a starving rattler. Some call him "The Hunter"; he likes to turn men loose, sometimes, track 'em down and use 'em for target practice.'

'My God! Did Lafe threaten you with Squires?'

'Yeah, I guess he did.'

'And it doesn't bother you?'

'If you mean "worry" me, no, not much. I already know Squires has been hired to kill me. Only thing that bothers me is *when* he'll make his try, and how.'

'Won't he challenge you?'

Matt smiled wryly. 'Aw, he'll find some excuse to call me out. Squires likes an audience best, so I reckon he won't try to dry-gulch me out on the range. It'll be in town, with plenty of folk to watch.'

'How – how can you be so – so damn *casual?*' She slapped a hand against the veranda post.

119

'I'm not. I'll be ready for him.'

She heaved a sigh. 'You think you can outdraw him?'

'Reckon not.'

'Then damnit, Matt! My question stands!'

'Look, Eadie, I know Squires is here to kill me. He won't do it till I leave here. He'll even give me a couple of days' grace to get my legs under me again after laying-up in bed. See? He won't want folk to say afterwards he gunned me down when I was weak and not fully recovered. He'll want it to look all fair and square, and there's nothing I can do to change those things. I just have to be ready to do the best I can when the time comes.'

She regarded him soberly, still frowning. 'I – I've never known a man quite like you, Matt Dawson.'

'I'm nothing special. But talking about men you've known: were you ever married?'

She stiffened, startled. 'Yes. My husband, Dave, died three years ago. A runaway wagon – he snatched a child out of the way, threw her clear, but he fell under the wheels. That was in Laredo. What made you ask?'

'I'm sorry if I stirred sad memories, but—' He held up the geological survey map, folded and creased. 'You wrote your name on the back: "Edith Kern, nee Durham". . . .'

She smiled. 'I – Dave sent for that map for me. I get – sentimental at times. It's the "Durham" you want to know about, isn't it?'

'Well, "Durham Bend" and so on. . . .'

'Yes, the original settler after the Spanish Grant was

finally broken up into lots was my grandfather, Asa Durham. He settled about where Box K is now, by the bend of the river. I remember him as a kind man. I was only five when he died, but he made an impression on me.' She paused, then added in a quieter voice, 'Actually, you remind me of him: strong, tough, scruples you don't like to admit to; a clear sense of fair play, if you like.'

'You got me mixed up with someone else.' He smiled. 'Your grandfather is why you wanted to buy Luke's land?'

'Yes, another silly sentimental notion I had at the time. There was a small annuity from an insurance policy that Dave had taken out. I don't think Luke really wanted to sell but Randall was giving him such a hard time that he agreed to my price, which was only just over half of what Randall offered. I believe that's what got him killed: Lafe took it as a personal insult.'

'Why does Randall want your place? He's got better and bigger pastures, the water's just as plentiful. Is he just greedy for more land?'

Her face was sober as she studied him for a long moment. Eventually she said, 'I think you've opened a can of worms there. I've often puzzled over Lafe's reasons.'

Matt had been walking along the veranda for short distances for the last couple of days, and although his shoulder still hurt and was restricted in its movement, he could feel his body recovering well.

Now he got out of the cane wheelchair before she could come to his aid and went to a small table at the far end of the veranda, where he had some magazines and the folded Spanish map of the original Grant.

'With time on my hands, I've been amusing myself trying to match the Spanish map and its freehand style to the Survey chart. I think I can find several locations, like here, on the river bend. On the Spanish map it's drawn too far in from what has to be the Organ Pipes. But if it was where I reckon it should be – about here – it's a good starting point for working out other locations.'

'Ye-es, I can see that. Always supposing the river bend is where you think it should appear.'

He placed a finger on the chart. 'I place it here, where it runs close along your south-west line.'

She nodded, willing to agree but mystified as to what he was getting at. She looked even more bewildered when he tapped the crude illustration on the Spanish chart that showed what he believed to be the entrance of a mine shaft.

'Could that be any kind of a landmark on your land? Say a cairn of rocks that might look natural after all this time? Or just a deep dent in the hillside, over-grown. . . ?'

'It looks like a shored-up mine entrance or it could be part of a log cabin. . . .' She shook her head. 'No, there's nothing like that. I've never heard of anyone mining for gold or silver out here.'

'Not recently, no, but the Spaniards did a lot of searching for gold and silver, rubies and other precious stones. Everywhere they went teams were sent out to look for any clues that might lead to riches.'

He paused and then told her about his theory concerning the nature of the injuries of the men who had died.

'Doc agrees they could've been hurt in a cave-in. I worked for you long enough to know that part just beyond the bend of the river on your land. A high bank, fairly steep, as if it had been cut that way—'

'By floods, surely.'

'No. It looks too vertical for that; floods would undermine it. I think it was dug away. I talked with Julia's fiancé who said he'd worked for Randall not too long ago.'

'Will Severin? Yes, Will's a fencing contractor. Lafe hired him to run a fence across that area a while back, not long before Luke Rafter sold to me!'

'Yeah, and he saw what could be the entrance to a tunnel, one that was being worked on. Randall said it was only where they had started to dig a dam, but he changed his mind.'

'No one here needs a dam this close to the river. Oh, you think Randall was starting a tunnel. But what for? To search for some old Spanish mine?'

Dawson nodded. 'I reckon that tunnel's been dug, well into the side of the hill by now, and part of it collapsed on those three men they brought here to Doc's.'

She looked hard at both maps, tracing a line below the river bend with her finger.

'If that's the area, it's very close to my line.'

'*That*'s what I'm getting at, Eadie. Suppose there are traces of gold there and Randall's men are following it towards a mother lode, or looking for a rich vein?'

She frowned down at the map again, then turned her head sharply towards him. 'But if they did that, they'd soon be across my line and digging under my land!'

Smiling faintly he nodded. 'Yeah, and what if they find the main vein or the motherlode – on your land?'

He heard her breath suck in sharply. She seemed to hold it before speaking in a whisper, 'Then – would it be my gold? Or Randall's. . . ?'

'There's no question, Eadie. The gold would be yours. The only way Randall could get it would be to steal it without you knowing. Or drive you off Box K.'

He could see she was a little excited now. 'I certainly don't know of any tunnel being dug under Box K!'

'There may not be, but I think it's possible, and that's why Randall wants you off your spread. Hiring those men to stampede your herd, and so on.'

She was silent long enough for him to roll and light a cigarette. Then she smiled.

'You have been busy, Matt!'

'Amusing myself. I can't claim any more than that, Eadie, but I've a hunch I might be right.'

Suddenly, she stiffened and looked at him almost in alarm.

'What is it?'

'I've just remembered! My grandfather gave my father a small nugget of gold to wear on his watch chain. He just said he "found" it and hoped it would bring the family good luck. It didn't, but that's not the point, is it? I don't know what happened to the nugget, but I wonder whether he found it on his land?'

'Now your land. I guess it's possible, and if it is, so is my theory about the tunnel.'

'I'll go take a look? I can always say I'm checking the pasture for a new fence line. . . .'

'Don't, and don't send Spanish or Alec, and sure not young Curly. Randall's hired this Tully Squires and that shows he's ready to kill if he has to. He's already turned Link Hauser loose on me, but this time he's brought in a real pro.'

'And we no longer have a lawman in Durham!'

'No. If you were caught nosing around that area, you'd probably meet with some kind of fatal "accident".'

He watched the blood drain from her face, leaving it white and pinched.

CHAPTER 11

NEW LAW

The next morning when Doc Fallon made his usual visit he brought three townsmen with him. Dawson knew one was Bondurant, the general store owner, and another was a kind of mystery man named Kildare – it was said he owned the saloon and its gambling concession as well as the cat house over the creek in what they called the 'Tenderloin' district of Durham Bend; a 'silent' partner with Tate Meehan.

The third man was Judge Bradley McClannahan, a hook-nosed, lantern-jawed hulk who looked more like a retired mountain man than a respected member of the judiciary.

Fallon got straight to the point.

'Matt, you know these gentlemen – by sight if not personally.' They all nodded or murmured and Dawson gave a short acknowledgement to each. 'These, along with myself, comprise the Durham Town

Council. We like to think we have the welfare of the entire County at heart, though, and so far we've been re-elected twice.'

'Must be doin' something right, then,' Dawson allowed, still wondering why they were here.

'We like to think so. Judge? Would you care to put our request to Matt here?'

The big judge wrinkled his hooked nose, drew out a kerchief and blew into it noisily before speaking as he replaced the kerchief in his coat pocket.

'We need a man to replace Lyndon Britt, Dawson. Lyndon was a good man as far as he was able, but he was keeping poorly and getting worse as he got older. His reputation, of course, carried him through, and probably got him killed in the end. Being back-shot, I mean.'

'I see where you're heading, Judge, but I must decline the offer.'

'Now, wait up, Matt,' the doctor said quickly. 'You'll be out of here in a day or so. I know your shoulder won't be fully back to normal movement for perhaps another week, but it's not your gun arm – and, to be honest, it's guns we're worried about.'

'Doc means that killer Lafe Randall has brought in,' said Bondurant, making munching movements with his mouth; he claimed it was caused by ill-fitting dentures he'd ordered by mail from Denver. 'Tully Squires. The man couldn't notch his gunbutt if he tried! It'd whittle it clear away from what we've heard.'

'Exaggeration, Doc,' Dawson said, smiling faintly. 'He is a killer, but Randall'll keep him out on the range. That's where he wants him.'

'And he can ride in any time and lift the lid off this town,' the judge snapped in his gravelly voice. 'We're a law-abiding town, Dawson. We don't have gunfighters here. Any time this Squires gets a load of redeye under his belt and turns nasty, it'll be our citizens who feel his wrath, and that means dead men, with a man like Squires.'

Dawson looked at them each in turn. 'What makes you think I could stand up against Squires? I'm no gunfighter.'

'You have a certain toughness about you, Matt; courage, if you like,' Fallon told him quietly. 'I'm not buttering you up, but almost everyone who's met you says the same thing. You know what is right and you stand up for folk. We know you're honest because of how you brought in Luke Rafter's body and his horse, when you could've just as easily ridden off and left him for the coyotes. There are other things, but we won't prolong this. We want you as town marshal, Matt, and here "town" means the county as well, being so isolated out here. The pay's good, you'll have either a room at the hotel or a small cabin on the edge of town that Britt used for living quarters.'

The others put in their two-cents' worth, too, and Dawson ended up frowning and making an exasperated gesture with his good arm.'Quit it, will you, gents? Can't stand a bunch of voices all aimed at me. Let me think it over. Just now I'm still on Eadie Kern's payroll and she has a few problems of her own I feel oligated to help with.'

'See?' Bondurant cut in, addressing his colleagues. 'That's the kind of man we want in the law office! One with a sense of responsibility.'

'Definitely,' said Fallon emphatically.

'I agree,' added the judge. 'Loyalty—'

' "Rides for the brand", I believe is the term.'

They all looked at Kildare, who had remained silent up until now. 'If you don't want the law job, Matt, I can sure use you managing the gambling concession. I reckon the present man is skimming the takings off the top—'

'Damnit, Race!' snapped the judge. 'This isn't recruitment of men for your establishments! Personally, I didn't want you along on this, and, anyway, you're out of order.'

Kildare, urbane, better dressed than the others, took a drag on the factory-made cigarette he was smoking in an ivory-and-silver holder, smiling slowly. He winked at Dawson. 'I'll pay double what the marshal's job will—'

'Race!' snapped Bondurant. 'I think you better go!'

Fallon and the judge agreed. Kildare rose slowly from his chair and bowed slightly. 'Gentlemen. We'll see each other at the next council meet, unless you are inclined to visit my . . . establishments; is that what you called 'em, Judge? I often see you there, so. . . .'

The councillors worked hard at keeping straight faces as Kildare left, and Fallon turned back to Dawson. 'You wouldn't consider his offer over ours, would you, Matt?'

'Tempting!' Dawson said and couldn't help smiling

at the looks of consternation. 'Relax. I said I'd think about the marshal's job and I will, but you've got to realize that if I take that badge it won't scare Tully Squires. 'Fact, it could make him try even harder to shoot it out with me on Main. A marshal going down to him would boost his reputation through the roof.'

'But – but you could handle Squires, couldn't you?' Even as he asked, the worry and uncertainty showed on Bondurant's face.

'You want an honest answer, and of course you do, then I have to say 'I doubt it'. I'm no gunslinger.'

'My God! But you're our only hope!'

'Contact the federal marshal's office; there's one in Austin. They'll send a man who's trained for the work.'

The trio eventually left him, shaking their heads, disappointment obvious. Doctor Fallon delayed, but after one look at Dawson's face he sighed and followed the other councillors.

Dawson rolled a cigarette and smoked it thoughtfully.

Curly Knox hauled rein and even let the boisterous heifer he was chasing escape into some brush and head back into Box K, such was his surprise. He stood in the stirrups and stared down at the ground a few yards in front, the sight that had made him skid his chestnut gelding to a halt.

When he was a kid – well, perhaps, when he was younger might be more fitting – he remembered his big brother Reece taking him, on a dare, to the local boot hill in the Mississippi town where they were living. At midnight.

'I'll show you where the dead'uns rise outta their graves and go through the town lookin' for someone to scare,' Reece had told young Curly. 'An' *eat 'em up*!'

'I – I don't wanna see!'

'Aah, you're a real 'fraidy-cat, Curly! I dunno why I stick up for you when the kids poke fun at you. Look, you come with me to the cemetery at midnight and I'll spread the word. They won't fun you all the time then.'

'Can't you just say I was with you?'

'Nooooo. You come and I'll tell everyone how you wasn't scared.'

Of course they were both scared, but Reece covered his fear much better than young Curly. But it was a let-down, anyway.

All Reece could find were two or three really old graves that had started to sink in the middle, short, scoop-like troughs where the earth had subsided.

'That's how they start!' Reece said, trying desperately now to convince his no-longer-scared kid brother that this was where the ghosts escaped their earthy confinement.

Curly ended up scaring Reece by running away, hiding behind a tree and, when the bigger boy came searching, jumping out, flinging arms wildly and making blood-curdling screams.

Boy! That was a story he told a hundred times and Reece and his friends no longer called him scaredy-cat.

131

What he was looking at now, holding the restless chestnut in check, were elongated, sunken streaks in the ground ahead, like those he'd seen in that cemetery years ago. Three troughs of varying lengths, the longest perhaps ten feet, the shortest six.

What was more, he knew what they meant; Eadie had called the crew together and told them about Dawson's tunnel theory and ordered them to stay clear of the Box K line where it was anywhere near Rocking R's land. If Randall thought they were nosing around and there really was a tunnel, there would be more trouble than you could shake a stick at.

But in his excitement to catch the runaway heifer, Curly had actually crossed the invisible boundary line and was now on Randall land. What was more, by moving the chestnut just a shade closer, he could see where there was a big pile of dirt that had obviously been dug out of the hillside, the earth raw and even a spade stuck in it at an angle.

There was a tunnel! And this was where it had collapsed! The roof in this section hadn't fully fallen in, but enough of the supporting earth, and likely rotten beams and posts, had given way and dragged down the surface into these trough-like shapes above ground.

Matt Dawson was right! Randall had been digging a tunnel under the line, on to Box K land! If it hadn't collapsed they might never have known.

'You're trespassin', kid.'

Curly's stomach jumped up into his throat and he gave a small cry at the sound of the voice behind and slightly above him. A man stood beside a bush, Colt cocked and covering him. Curly recognized him as one of Randall's cowboys, only a little older than himself; they had sometimes met in town on payday and had a mild wingding.

'Judas, Mort! I damn near wet my pants, you scarin' me like that! I was chasin' a heifer but it got away from me.'

'If it run on to Rocking R, it belongs to us now.'

'Hey! That ain't fair! Miss Eadie'll have somethin' to say about that, and so'll Matt Dawson!'

'That busted-up drifter? Hell, he don't scare me, not now we got Tully Squires as a sidekick.'

Curly swallowed. 'Well, I don't want no trouble, Mort. I don't see the heifer so I'll just ride on back to Box K, and Miss Eadie can sort it out with Randall.'

Mort grinned without humour. 'Uh-uh. You come with me. You're gonna meet Tully Squires in person.'

'Aw, come on, Mort! I don't want nothin' to do with that killer. Listen, I bought you a drink last payday!'

'I 'preciate that, Curl, but I work for Mr Randall so you stay put, hands raised like that while I come on down an' whistle up my own hoss. We're takin' a short ride.'

'Why you doin' this?'

Mort grinned. 'Want to see your face when you meet Tully.'

' "Tully", huh? Like you're friends?' scoffed Curly and started to turn the chestnut. But he checked when Mort's gun hammer snicked back to full cock. 'Judas! What's wrong with you?'

'Let's go, Curl. Time I got myself into Randall's

good books. He's lookin' for a new top hand.'

'Well, don't 'spect no more free drinks from me, you damn snitch!'

Curly did as he was told, wishing he could find the courage to try to escape. It wasn't that he wouldn't fight, but he knew he was slow with firearms and had no chance if the treacherous Mort really did want to shoot him.

When he saw Tully Squires with Randall down the slope, staring at a vast length of collapsed earthbank, behind which had been the tunnel, he knew he was no braver now than when Reece first took him into the midnight graveyard.

Mort quickly told his story and Randall swore. 'You damn fool! Should've just sent him on his way. Now he's seen the tunnel! Get the hell back to work!'

'I – I won't say nothin', Mr Randall,' Curly assured him. Tully Squires laughed as the crestfallen Mort turned his mount away and rode off slowly.

'You sound real scared, kid. Bet you feel like runnin' – and bet you can leave a courtin' jackrabbit like he was standin' still once you get gain', huh?'

Curly smiled nervously. 'Well, I can run pretty good, but—'

'That's what I want to hear.' Squires turned to the puzzled Randall. 'Turn him loose.'

'Like hell! I said he's seen the *tunnel*—'

'Don't mean he'll tell anyone about it.' Squires set his cold smile in Curly's direction. 'I need a little target practice. Turn him loose and we'll play hidy-go-seek up in them trees for a while. Suit you, kid?'

Curly felt his stomach heave.

It was the day Dawson had been looking forward to for over a week. Doc Fallon had at last given the OK for his discharge. He had exercised his shoulder – and his body – to a programme set up by Julia and Fallon himself. He was feeling good, impatient to be out and about, earned the doctor's wrath with his endless query: When am I gonna be released from this prison, Doc?

The answer: 'When I consider you're ready – and not before. You're not a very good patient, you know!'

'I know! Because I'm fit enough now not to be a goddamn patient!'

'Wait!'

There was nothing else he could do, and now, this day, this wonderful, glorious, sunny day, it appeared he had at last made the grade and was about to be discharged.

'But only if you give me your word you'll continue to do those exercises. Do them every day for three weeks, then come see me. You do like I say and you'll get full motion, painless motion, back into that shoulder.'

Dawson lifted the arm, felt the grind of healing bones, the wrenching pain of damaged muscles. But he kept his face blank. 'Feels good already, Doc.'

'You do those exercises or you'll never regain full movement!'

'OK, OK!' Agree to anything to get out of here.

Fallon examined the healing wound and turned to

Julia. 'We'll put the arm in a sling. I think the less movement the better.'

'Now, wait up, Doc! A sling?'

'A sling,' Fallon told him flatly. 'Make it that square of black silk, Julia, that the undertaker gave us. You'll at least have a bit of style, Matt! And I think we might make a plaster cast of the shoulder and set it under the bandage, just for further protection.'

'Why not get me a suit of armour!'

'Good idea, but I don't know where to find one.'

As Dawson sat resignedly while Julia fashioned the sling, and the doctor smeared the plaster over the webbing of bandages encircling his triceps and shoulder, Fallon asked, 'Given any more thought to the marshal's job?'

'Can't make up my mind, Doc. Don't really want it, I like this town and it's treated me pretty good, but I just haven't decided yet.'

'We'd like a decision as soon as possible, Matt.'

As it happened he wasn't discharged that day; Doc Fallon decided he should remain overnight while the plaster set in place over his high upper arm and the point of his shoulder, which needed protection because of a chip of bone. He had to keep as still as possible. Matt Dawson was not a pleasant person when he awoke for his breakfast.

But around about mid-morning, arm in the sling now, the plaster cap resting protectively on the damaged limb, and surprisingly comfortable, the medic said he could leave.

'I'm grateful, Doc. Sorry I was such a sorehead.'

'You're not the first I've had to deal with and I'm sure you won't be the last. Plenty of movement in that arm?'

Dawson nodded, demonstrated that he could move his left arm about two-thirds as good as it should be.

'We-eell, I don't know. . . .' Fallon began and then could hide his smile no longer as he saw Dawson's eyes widen, then pinch down, hot with rising anger. 'Oh, I suppose it won't hurt to turn you loose.'

'I can guarantee it'll hurt not to, Doc!'

Then there were the sounds of some kind of commotion outside and someone called for 'the doctor!' Fallon hurried out, Julia tied off the knot on the sling and went after him.

Matt Dawson began gathering his things, mostly one-handed, but pleased with the amount of movement he had in his left arm. Then he heard tramping boots and many voices. Stuffing gear into one of his saddle-bags, he looked up as the door opened and a whole bunch of men – and women – tried to squeeze into the small infirmary.

Two of them laid a blood-spotted tarp on the bed, lifted one flap, and revealed the body of young Curly Knox.

'Goddlemighty!' someone breathed with both reverence and revulsion. 'The kid's been shot to pieces! Must have at least a dozen bullet wounds. . . !'

Dawson pushed through and stared down at the dead cowhand. 'Tully Squires,' he said heavily, and as folk stared at him, added, 'One of his trade marks: likes to turn a man loose and hunt him down like an animal. Only they have nothing to fight back with.'

Fallon shook his head. 'Murder, pure and simple! Four of those bullets are in Curly's back.' He swivelled his gaze to Dawson, who was looking at a young cowboy in the second row of the crowd: one of the men who had carried Curly in. He had tears streaking through the dirt on his face. Matt thought he worked for Lafe Randall, Mort or Curt, some name like that. As the cowboy swung away, the doctor's voice got Dawson's attention.

'Matt. . . ?'

Dawson tightened his mouth, nodded briefly,

'You just got yourself a marshal, Doc.'

CHAPTER 12

CHALLENGE

Somehow the crowd of gawkers was hustled outside and Dawson reached the porch as Bondurant stepped up and said,

'I think the sooner we have you sworn in the better, Matt.'

'Whatever you say.' Matt was moving his gaze over the crowd, and was surprised to see Randall and a bunch of his men on the fringes, including Tully Squires. ' 'Fact, if the judge is handy. . . .'

Judge McClannahan arrived within minutes and minutes later Matt Dawson was officially marshal of Durham Bend and the surrounding county. By that time, too, Eadie had arrived with Spanish and Alec Crewe.

'Where is he, Doctor?' Eadie barely glanced at Matt at first and then saw the marshal's badge Bondurant had pinned to his shirtfront. Her eyes met his. 'I trust you'll be arresting someone for this – this atrocity!'

'Reckon so, Eadie.'

He pushed through the crowd, favouring his arm in the sling and stopped in front of Tully Squires.

'Got your name all over it, Tully.'

'What're you talkin' about? You mean that poor kid that walked in front of our guns?'

Matt stiffened. The crowd fell utterly silent. Randall smirked but said nothing.

'Tell me,' Matt said to Squires.

'Well, Lafe there was gettin' worried with you killin' so many of his men. He figured I should give his crew some hints on shootin'. You know, to protect themselves. We went up into the foothills and I set up targets, then I took 'em into the brush as that's a different kinda shootin'. You likely know that.'

'I know you killed Curly, no matter what story you're making up.'

Tully spread his arms innocently. 'Hey! You can't pin this on me! Hell, see them four men with Lafe? They was with me and we had a whole slew of targets lined up on a deadfall. About to shoot when this damn heifer come runnin' through. We let it go and just as we started shootin' this kid come outta nowhere, obviously chousing the heifer. I yelled to cease fire but it was too late.' He paused, shook his head. 'Nothin' we could do. I'm sure sorry about it but it was just one of them things.'

Before Dawson could answer, and while the crowd were murmuring, Randall stepped forward and confronted the new marshal.

'See you're makin' this official. Well, what Tully told you was what happened.' He gestured to his crew and they stepped forward. Mort Day wasn't one of them. 'You fellers tell the marshal.'

They did, all speaking at once at first, then individually. Each explained, almost word for word, the same story as Squires had told.

'There y'are,' Tully said, with a mirthless grin, staring challengingly at Dawson. He moved his gaze to the pale-faced, stiff-bodied Eadie, walked across and held out some money he had taken from his pocket. 'It's about all I can do now, ma'am, but maybe you can get a sorta headboard for the kid; sure was mighty bad luck.'

Eadie put a lot of contempt into her look as she slapped his hand aside, the bills spilling from Squires's fingers. She said nothing; it wasn't necessary.

The crowd went very silent. Squires nodded gently and picked up his money. He tucked it away into his shirt pocket, unsmiling, touched his other hand to his hatbrim.

'Sorry you feel that way, ma'am.'

Eadie, eyes brimming, turned away quickly.

'Well, nothin' we can do here now, Lafe,' Tully said, hitching at his gunbelt, gaze briefly touching Dawson's rocky face. 'Might's well head back to Rockin' R, I guess.'

'Not you, Tully.'

Squires was turning away; he stopped the movement abruptly, snapped his head around towards the marshal. 'What?'

141

He stiffened when he saw Dawson was holding his six-gun in his good hand, hammer cocked back. The hastily drawn-in collective sigh of the crowd seemed to hang in the suddenly still air.

'The hell're you doing?' demanded Randall, stepping forward. 'Damnit, we've explained what happened; my crew admitted it was their guns that brought down the kid, Tully told you. *It was an accident!*'

'I've seen him in action. He likes to turn loose some unarmed ranny in the brush, give him a start, then hunt him down.'

'Christ, man, that rumour's been doin' the rounds for years!' Randall snapped. 'Man with a fast-gun rep-utation like Tully always has some wild story like that circulatin'. . . .'

'But it's true. I know a man lost a pard that way.' Dawson looked coldly at Squires. 'Larry McGrew. Irishman with only half an ear.'

Tully stared back, then said, low-voiced and with a crooked smile, 'Was that the sonuver's name? Carried a hidden knife that missed. Nearly nailed me.'

'So you shot him with the gun muzzle against his neck; almost blew his head off. You'd already wounded him three times, before you finished the poor bastard.'

'Like everythin' else, you got it wrong. I never—'

'Shut up! Doc, would you take Tully's gun. From behind! Don't get between me and him.'

Squires, his face ugly now, a murderous look in his eyes, lifted his hands slowly. 'You ain't locking me up!'

'Law office to your left. I'll be right behind you.'

Matt picked two townsmen to accompany him and held his gun on Squires until the cell door clanged shut and the key turned in the lock. The townsmen were eager to get away. Tully sat on the bunk. When he realized there was only Dawson in the cell block passage, he said bleakly,

'I'll enjoy killin' you more'n I have killin' anyone for years, Dawson.'

'Think about it, Tully. Because that's all you'll be able to do – before you stretch a rope.'

Squires stood up and ran at the bars, knuckles white where his hands gripped them. Dawson was walking back towards the front of the building. Tully cut loose with a mouthful of filthy epithets and threats but Matt merely closed the connecting door to the office behind him and locked it.

When he turned round he dropped the keys and whipped a hand to his six-gun, had it almost clear of leather before he recognized Mort Day standing in the shadow of the gun cabinet, nervous and pinch-faced. The kid hastily set down a derringer he had been holding; there was an open desk drawer so Matt figured the gun had come from it.

'What're you doing with that, Mort? That belonged to Marshal Britt. Saved his life once, he told me.'

The cowboy nodded, glanced through the dusty window. 'I – I wasn't takin' it, honest. It's just that . . . they took my six-gun and I wanted some sorta protection.'

'Who's "they"? You got something to tell me, Mort?'

143

'Randall still out there?' Dawson nodded and Mort licked his lips. 'I never meant no harm to come to Curly. I was showin' off when I seen him chase that heifer on to Rockin' R land.'

Nervously, he told Matt about his meeting with Curly and because Randall had vaguely said he'd consider promoting him to top hand he felt kind of big-headed and swaggered some; he made Curly ride to where Randall and his men were working near the tunnel.

'We – we always had a kinda rivalry, you know? Crew of Rockin' R and crew of Box K, Curly an' me in partic'lar. I was showin' off. Just meant it for a bit of fun. Throw a scare into old Curly.'

'Well, you got it wrong, Mort.'

'Lafe and Tully took Curly up into the foothills.' After a while, there was a lot of shootin'.'

'Those cowboys with Randall outside – did they go into the foothills, too? When Tully took Curly, I mean?'

'No. Not till the shootin' stopped.'

After Tully had hunted down Curly.

'You testify to this, Mort?'

Mort shook his head quickly. 'They'd kill me. Just wanted you to know. I feel real bad about Curly.'

He was edging around the big desk and Dawson frowned. He opened the gun cabinet and held a Colt out towards the scared cowboy. 'Here's some protection for you. It's not loaded but you've got your bullet belt. I need your testimony, Mort, to nail Tully Squires. If you'll—'

'Sorry, Marshal!' Mort snatched the gun and

ducked round the desk, backed to the rear door which was open. He ran out into the yard to his saddled mount by the sagging fence way down past the stablese. Panting, Matt watched helplessly while Mort leapt into the saddle and spurred away.

He was glad the cowboy had told him what had happened, but he would have liked Mort to stick around and tell the same story in the witness box.

In the street, the crowd had strolled along closer to the law office now and Randall swaggered through, pushing citizens roughly aside.

'You can't do this, Dawson! You got witnesses tellin' you what happened! You better turn Tully loose.'

'You keep flapping your mouth, I'll lock you up as a material witness.'

That wiped the smile off Randall's face and the real anger he had been holding in suddenly burst out. 'You're a goddamned liar! All these things you reckon you've done, places you've been. You'd have to be about seventy years old to have to've managed 'em.'

'I've managed.' And Matt took a sudden step forward and backhanded Randall across the mouth. The big man staggered, from shock as much as hurt, though blood smeared across his chin. 'And I don't take kindly to anyone calling me a liar.'

Randall began to straighten, instinctively reaching for his gun, but Matt was already covering him with his Colt. The rancher paled slightly, then snapped.

'I oughta punch your teeth in!' Randall gritted wiping blood from his mouth with a kerchief, eyes blazing.

'Couldn't do it, even if I've only got one arm.'

Suddenly Randall grinned. 'Hey! I could lick you with one hand tied behind my back! You game?'

'Matt, no!' called Eadie from a couple of rows back in the crowd, sensing that it was the kind of challenge Dawson would accept; couldn't afford not to in front of the crowd. 'Doc! Doc Fallon! Don't let him do this. . . .'

But Matt had already decided. 'Right here and now.'

Eadie dragged Fallon through the crowd and they stepped in front of the marshal. 'Matt, please don't be so foolish!' the girl implored him.

'Foolish isn't the word,' Fallon said curtly. 'You accept this challenge, it'll be plain idiocy! Matt, you'll probably ruin that shoulder.'

'You've got it protected with plaster, Doc.' Matt was already slipping the arm out of the sling. 'Someone get a rope and strap this arm to my side,' he said, ignoring the medic's protests and those of Eadie.

The crowd were getting excited now; this would be something to see! Randall had loosened his trouser belt and thrust his left arm through, pulled it tight and one of his men buckled it. Randall looked coldly at Dawson who was testing the rope one of the crowd had wrapped about his body to hold his injured arm immobile. He ignored the discomfort, glanced towards Randall.

At the same instant the crowd roared and Dawson tried to jump aside, but was too late. Randall lunged without warning, turning his shoulder into Dawson's chest, following swiftly with a looping blow from his right. The fist skidded along Dawson's jaw, snapped his head back, and tore at the tendons running from his neck to his wounded shoulder. He grunted aloud in pain, took another blow just beneath the wound and felt his rage surge; Randall was going for the wound!

The rancher kept bulling his way forward and Dawson felt the front row of the crowd at his back. Hands thrust him forward, some tried to pull him aside as the angry rancher stomped after him, swinging and swearing.

At last Matt went down, off balance with only one arm to swing. When he fell, Randall was on him instantly, kicking and stomping. Boot heels drove into his lower legs, hard leather toes thudded into his thighs, numbing the muscles. One drove at his crotch and he instinctively rolled, drawing up his legs, taking the blow on his buttock. It hurt and when he continued his roll, head down, knees under him, he couldn't get enough strength in his legs to lunge upright.

Instinct made him flop on to his left side. He gritted his teeth against the pain in his bad arm, the searing heat knifing into his shoulder. He got on to his back and as Randall stumbled in, feeling off-balance too, Dawson lifted his boots into the man's belly. The rancher grunted, gagged, and doubled over. Matt squirmed into position and then thrust up, turning his left shoulder a little so the plaster cast beneath the shirt and bandages took Randall in the face.

Nose and mouth smashed, teeth breaking off,

Randall floundered back like a crazy drunk in his attempt to keep his feet. He was hurt badly. Dawson fell on his knees, gasping, but staggered upright, wobbly and unsteady. Randall was game and, though hurting badly, spitting blood, roared and charged in, hitting Dawson with his full, solid weight.

Matt was thrown back into the crowd, fell amongst hurrying boots as they tried to get out of the way. He snatched at a man's leg with his good hand, pulling himself up as the owner protested and tried to shake him off.

Randall came in again, swinging his boots. Matt side-stepped, kicked the leg that was meant to drive a boot into his belly and Randall staggered. He began to straighten, his face a mask of blood. Then his eyes widened as he stared unbelievingly: Matt Dawson had launched himself bodily and was hurtling at him, completely airborne.

Both Dawson's boots took Randall in the upper chest and hurled him back a good six feet. He crashed across the boardwalk, barely conscious. Dawson weaved across, lifted a boot above that blood-streaked face. . . .

'Matt! No!'Eadie screamed, hands going to her face. Dawson heard and reluctantly diverted the down-stomping boot just it time. It thudded into the boardwall. He drew it back again, a short ten inches, and kicked Randall in the head. Swaying with fatigue, he rested his boot across the dazed rancher's throat.

The victor. He was aware of the impression it would make on the townsfolk, though he felt a mite embarrassed, especially as he was swaying unsteadily on his feet, legs trembling from his exertions. Some victor!

Then Randall was stirring, his men helping him to his feet. The crowd were looking at Matt differently now; it was the first time they had ever seen Lafe Randall bested in a fight – and a one-armed one at that!

Somehow, the rancher didn't look so big and frightening as he had twenty minutes earlier. Nor would he, ever again in Durham Bend.

Matt didn't recall Eadie leading him to Doc Fallon's, but he sat there in the infirmary with the sawbones and Julia working on his bruised and battered shoulder.

'Of all the damn fools I've seen – and I've seen hundreds in my time – you take the cake, Matt!'

'It was just something that needed doing.' He tried to stifle a yawn without success. Eadie and Fallon looked at him, shaking their heads slowly.

'You'll stay here overnight.'

'No, Doc. I've got to sleep at the jail with Tully in the cell block.'

'Matt, you're pushing things too hard, man! You're tough but all you've been through has taken plenty out of you. *No*! Don't argue! You're going to get a good night's rest – right here!'

Dawson swallowed his retort: he hadn't seen the sawbones so riled before. Then Eadie said, 'Spanish and Alec can take it in turns at the jailhouse, Matt.'

He glared, but said nothing; he knew when he was beaten.

CHAPTER 13

MANHUNT

Spanish had the second shift, midnight to dawn.

It was barely full daylight when the rested Dawson walked into the law office and found him slumped at the desk. A coffee cup was lying on its side, brown liquid staining most of the papers scattered there.

Matt, his arm neatly slung again, face stiff and bruised, stepped forward quickly and felt for a neck pulse. Spanish was alive – and sleeping deeply.

'Someone spiked your java, Spanish!' he said grimly. He drew his six-gun and hurried through to the celiblock.

The door of Tully Squires's cell stood wide open; the keys were still in the lock.

He fetched Doc Fallon, who examined the still unconscious Spanish and picked up the empty cup, sniffing it.

'Chloral hydrate. I keep some, but Lemuel Gunston, the druggist, has the main supply.' Looking levelly at Matt, he added, 'His daughter, Emily, works at the all-night diner; it's said she's attracted to the cook. . . .'

'And Eadie arranged with her to take coffee and a snack from the diner to Spanish and Alec during the night! Damnit, Doc!'

Matt hurried out. It took only a few minutes angry questioning of the tearful druggist's daughter to learn she had only delivered the snacks; she said the cook had prepared them.

Matt caught the man fumbling to get out through the back door. After one punch to the ribs he confessed that Randall had bribed him to drug the coffee with chloral hydrate supplied by the girl, who had taken the chance now to run off.

'You can't go after Squires alone, Matt!' Eadie protested when he came to the infirmary and asked Julia to bind up his left hand; he said he had hurt it during the fight and he thought a bone might be fractured and needed the support of a bandage. He opened his hand slowly and wiggled his fingers, his back to Eadie. Julia looked up into his eyes, and they locked gazes for a long moment. Then she reached for the bandages.

'Best to be sure,' she said.

'I'll never get a posse from this town to go after a killer like Tully Squires,' Matt told Eadie as Julia worked on his hand.

'Surely that's reason enough for you not to go!'

Matt rubbed the heavy-looking bandage Julia Fallon had wrapped around his left hand. 'I should've thought of Randall pulling something like this. It's my chore, Eadie. I'm responsible, no matter what Spanish says.'

And nothing any of them could say would make him change his mind.

He took his rifle when he rode out, but knew he would be at a disadvantage if he had to use it. He couldn't hold the forestock with his left hand, but maybe if he loosened the arm from the sling he could lift it high enough to rest the fore end across his arm steadily enough for an aimed shot. Maybe.

The fugitives hadn't tried to hide their trail and he rode warily, figuring that the clear sign was for his benefit, making it easy to follow, but they still managed to pull a fast one.

Tully Squires had somehow dropped out of the bunch and was suddenly sitting in the middle of the trail when Dawson rode his dun around a nest of boulders as high as a building. The marshal hauled on the reins, hurriedly rammed the leather between his teeth, but he was still too slow to get at his gun. His hand closed on it but Tully merely grinned mirthlessly and shook his head, waving his Colt once.

'Uh-uh, you son of a bitch! Got you right where I want you this time.'

Dawson fought the prancing horse, took the reins from between his teeth and got it settled down. 'No audience here, Tully.'

Squires's face clouded and for a moment Matt thought he was going to shoot. But he gained control and smiled that tight smile again. 'No, curse you! But I think I like this better. You let the reins dangle and lift the good arm high as it'll go. Don't try to move the bad one, keep it right still in that sling. Do it!'

Matt obeyed and Tully walked his mount close, coming in at right angles on Matt's right side. Then he reached out and flipped Dawson's Colt from the holster. He rammed the gun into his belt, backed up his horse, staying on that side.

'Climb down.'

'I need to lower my arm. . . .'

'Do whatever you have to do, but *climb down*!'

Dawson dismounted awkwardly and Tully slapped the dun on the rump. It jumped away with a snort, leaving the marshal standing there, facing half-away from the killer.

'See them hills? 'Course you do. Start walkin', run if you like. You got ten minutes from the time you reach the base of the foot hills. Then I'm comin' after you.'

'The usual set-up, eh? All the odds stacked in your favour.'

'You figure I'd give *you* a sportin' chance?' Tully laughed briefly. 'You gotta be loco! Now, get movin'.'

'Randall gonna help?' Matt asked, starting to jogtrot towards the brush-clad foothills.

'Lafe's givin' you to me as a gift!' Squires called, the rising pleasure he was feeling reflected in his voice. 'I'm a greedy cuss. Like to keep the good things to myself!'

He fired and the bullet kicked dust within inches of Dawson's right boot. He increased his pace, hearing

Squires's laughter gradually fading as he got in among the trees and brush. Being one-armed was a handicap. He was unable to thrust aside the head-high branches that swung into his face and had to duck awkwardly. They dragged across his hat, knocked it off twice.

After the second time, when he was picking it up, a gun blasted and he heard the lead carving its way through branches over his head. Tully Squires was an accurate gunman . . . *damn the luck!*

The climb up the slope was taking more out of him than he expected. Doc Fallon was right: that fight hadn't done him much good, even if he did win it. He stumbled and instinctively tried to put out his left hand to steady himself. It hurt like hell when he rammed it against a forked branch and quickly he pulled his arm back into the sling. His shoulder hurt too, and he turned so that he led with his good right side.

Behind and below he heard the brush crashing as Tully forced his mount through.

Hell! Seemed Squires was impatient, wasn't even hunting him down on foot! All advantages were sure stacked in Squires's corner.

This knowledge urged him on, and he drew on reserves he knew he had but hadn't called on in a long time. His legs ached and his boots slid and skidded on loose gravel, sometimes just on the steepness of the slope as he climbed higher. Squires spotted him every so often, fired at him, using a rifle and placing his shots carefully. He didn't aim to hit, not this early in the hunt. After each couple of shots, Matt heard the man laugh.

Once Tully called out: 'Won't be long now, Dawson! You ain't gonna make it to the crest, I'll tell you that.'

His breath was rasping and tearing at his throat and lungs, sweat was stinging his eyes, his wounded arm throbbed and his legs were turning to jelly; all this, and no six-gun.

He had been in better situations, and Tully was right. He wouldn't make it to the crest.

By now he was crawling up the steepest parts, gravel sliding under his groping right hand, tearing his fingernails and skin. Hell, even if he had a Colt, he'd be lucky to be able to shoot it with his hand all bloody, fingers stiff and torn.

There was a sudden rush from upslope. Tully, laughing like the fiend he was, charged down at him, running the sliding, snorting, wild-eyed horse at him. He must've dismounted, walked the horse through the trees which would screen it, then remounted and come charging down.

As Matt fell and began to slide, Tully threw down, triggering twice. The lead fanned Matt's face as he rolled to the side, yelling in pain as his bad arm folded beneath him. On his back, he deliberately started to slide on the loose scree, holding his bad arm across to his chest, his good hand covering the bandaged left one so as to hold it firmly.

It took Tully unawares and he had to pause and reload. By then Dawson had covered a deal of ground and was raising considerable dust as he plunged into the brush line below the trees.

Tully roared a curse and spurred his mount down,

crashing through the thicket, standing in the stirrups so as to get a better shot at Dawson.

He didn't want to kill him, not yet. No, sir: he wanted to wing the son of a bitch, keep him going until he was exhausted, lying at his feet, scarcely able to breathe, but conscious enough so he could see what was coming. Then he would shoot him to pieces like he had that kid, Curly.

He'd empty his own gun into him, then finish the job with Dawson's own Colt! Now that would be the perfect end!

He wrenched the reins suddenly as a dead branch rammed him in the chest with all Dawson's waning strength behind it. He went rolling over the horse's rump, wrenched from the saddle like a knight of old in a jousting match. The mount whickered and swerved, kept on going down the slope. Tully twisted and lost his six-gun. He snatched at a scrubby bush and stopped his fall.

He bared his teeth as he saw Dawson, most of his strength expended now, leaning against a tree trunk. His bad arm dangled straight down from the dislodged sling. Tully stood, breathing pretty hard himself, his chest bleeding from a ragged wound. He lifted Dawson's own Colt.

'See what – I got for – you!' He laughed. 'Your own gun! How you like – dem apples, huh? I'm gonna shoot pieces outta you with your own gun, and you'll die by the last bullet in it!'

'Don't – think so – I got somethin' – for you – too.'

'Yeah? What?' Tully asked with a sardonic laugh.

'This.'

Matt Dawson lifted his left arm with the heavily bandaged hand and the cloth suddenly erupted with a
spurt of flame. Tully Squires's head snapped back on
his neck as the derringer bullet took him between the
eyes.

He rolled down the slope and came to a stop at
Matt's feet. Dawson shook the bandaged hand; the
cloth was smouldering: the derringer shot had burned
his fingers. Lucky the small weapon had still been in
the desk drawer in the law office when he'd found
Spanish, and that Julia had immediately realized why
he had insisted his left hand be bandaged when he
had shown it to her. The derringer had been resting in
the palm of his hand, out of Eadie's line of vision.

After his breathing became more or less normal,
Matt tried to catch Tully's mount, but it had run off.
He eased his way down the slope and whistled up the
dun. He heard it trotting towards him and turned to
greet it.

But it wasn't his mount; it was Lafe Randall on his
big black, and there was a rifle in his right hand. He
reined up and lifted the weapon.

'You're a damn hard man to kill, Dawson! But this
is trail's end for you. Tully'll get the blame, so I got
nothin' to worry about.'

He raised the rifle to his shoulder and sighted carefully, though he couldn't possibly miss of such close
range.

Too near exhaustion to care now, Matt Dawson
leaned against a tree and waited for the kiling shot.

157

He heard the rifle crash, but no bullet tore into his body. He looked up quickly, in time to see Randall roll over his horse's rump and flop face down on the slope as the animal shied away. The rifle fell from his hand but there was no smoke curling from the barrel.

Then another horseman appeared, smoke curling from *his* Winchester that was resting butt-first on his left thigh.

Spanish nodded and half-smiled. 'I got such a damn hangover from that Mickey Finn it's a wonder I hit him.'

'I'm obliged,' Matt said, swaying. 'Thought you were still back at Doc's.'

Spanish shook his head. He dismounted and came to steady the marshal now. 'Hell no. I couldn't stay back there after lettin' you down like I did.'

'You didn't know they'd spiked your coffee.'

'Knew it when Doc told me. Had to come and square things, Matt.'

Dawson glanced at Randall's body. 'You did.'

Two weeks later Eadie sat her bay gelding a few feet away from where Matt Dawson stood beside his dun on the rise above the slope where the tunnel had collapsed.

'Guess we'll never know whether there was gold in there or not, now,' Eadie said. 'It'd be too dangerous to try to open up the tunnel again.'

'It could be done.'

'Not with safety, Matt. I wouldn't expect any man to work in dangerous conditions like that.'

'Easier than that.' Dawson smiled slowly. His arm was now out of its sling and he pointed to the heap of earth and rock at the tunnel mouth. 'You ever see that steam-donkey engine rusting away down behind the rail siding?'

'The. . .? Oh, yes, it's been there for over a year. They were thinking of starting a lumbermill and using it to drive the saws, but ran out of finance.' Her words were trailing off and she frowned a little. 'Why?'

'Well, that engine could be dismantled, brought up here and reassembled on that flatrock ledge just by the river bend; with a little work it could be converted into a pump, and with firehose and a needle nozzle like I saw in the firehouse in town, you could use a jet of water to wash that earth out. Then no one would be in danger if the tunnel did collapse.'

She stared, a little open-mouthed.

'If you reached the workface, you could use the same jet of water to flush out any gold that's there.' He saw she was still staring at him. 'It works, Eadie. I've done it, in an emerald mine in South America.'

Eadie suddenly smiled. 'Is there anything you haven't done, Matt Dawson?'

He smiled faintly, thinking about it, then said quietly, 'Never been married.'

She straightened, half-smiling. 'I'm – one up on you there, then.'

He nodded. 'Yeah. But mebbe it's about time I settled down, worked a spread of my own, counted cows for a change, instead of the dead.'

Her gaze held steadily to his face and she was silent,

159

only birdsong and the trickling of the river intruding.

'Count cows – or kids?' she asked at last.

After a moment, he said, 'How about: cows *and* kids?'

A smile lit up her tanned face.

'That's a better suggestion – a much better one.'